mojo hand

mojo hand

AN ORPHIC TALE

J. J. Phillips

CITY MINER ✕ BOOKS   BERKELEY

Originally published by Trident Press, a division of Simon & Schuster in 1966. Restored edition published by City Miner Books, P.O. Box 176, Berkeley, California 94701. 1985.

Cover is adapted from a photo of Coluber constrictor, the American blacksnake, provided by the New York Zoological Society, © New York Zoological Society. Back cover photo of author provided courtesy of Raleigh News and Observer.

Library of Congress Catalogue Card Number: 85-071335
ISBN: 0-933944-12-8

Cover Consultation: J.J. Phillips
Cover Design: Catherine Vandecasteele
Printed by McNaughton & Gunn in United States of America

10 9 8 7 6 5 4 3 2

contents

mojo hand

I'm going to Louisiana and get me a mojo hand
I'm going to Louisiana and get me a mojo hand
I'm going to show all you womens just how to fix your man.

Cold ground was my bed last night, rocks was my pillow, too
Cold ground was my bed last night, rocks was my pillow, too
You know I woke up this morning wondering what in the
    world am I going to do.

Don't let your man fix you like mine fixed me
Don't let your man fix you like mine fixed me
You know he make a fool about you, 'bout bad as a fool can be.

Now can't a man act funny, when he got another woman on
    his mind
Now can't a man act funny, when he got another woman on
    his mind
You know he drag his feet on the ground and he raising sand
    all the time.

I'm going in the morning, might not be gone but just one day
I'm going in the morning, might not be gone but just one day
When I bring my mojo back, that man going to do everything
    I say.

The new-dropped sun fell heavily to the ground by the Peppertree. The child was skipping rope when she saw it; the first thing she did was turn it over and pick it up. It was only about the size and weight of a basketball and looked like a ripe persimmon.

She held the warm ball close to her stomach, then carefully placed it back by the Peppertree and ran to Colonel Jim's Bait Store to borrow an old smelt bucket.

When she got back to the Peppertree, the sun was still there. The girl picked it up, pressed it to her stomach again, and laid it in the bucket. She walked to the screen door of the house and flattened her nose and forehead against it. She did not see her mother in the kitchen and she went in. She went to the stairs and started to go up when her father, who had been reading in the living room, came over to her.

"What are you doing with that old fish bucket?"

"I'm taking it to my room."

"Why?"

"I want to put it in my room for a while."

"What's in the bucket?"

"The sun."

"Oh, I see."

"No, it's really the sun. It fell by the Peppertree."

"Good God, it is the sun."

"I told you."

"Well, you can't keep the sun in a bucket. Get it out of here."

"I only wanted to keep it for tonight. Somebody does every night, and tonight is my turn."

"You cannot keep the sun in a bucket in your room. Get it out of the house."

"Well then, who will keep it if I don't?"

"I don't know, but I'm your father and I say you cannot keep it. Here, give me the bucket."

"All right."

Her father took the smelt bucket with the sun from her hand, put it carefully in the trunk of his car, drove the few blocks to the beach, and flung it in the surf. He put the rusty bucket back in the car and drove home.

The sun sizzled as it hit the water, turned red, and floated out to the horizon to drop off somewhere else.

J. J. P.
Wake County Jail
Raleigh, N.C.
August, 1962

part **one** *jelly, jelly*

one

Eunice got off the train from Lake Charles and stepped out into the station. The night was loud and steaming, it hung thick on everyone about the train station. The conductors and redcaps all moved slowly and when they called to one another their voices lost all strength, as if the words exhausted themselves in cutting through the dank night heat. The crowds were sparse, a few people here and there, thin men with seersucker shirts wet at the armpits, and fat women in faded housedresses. They stood in groups of three or four, not moving, merely scanning the people dropping down from the cars.

Occasionally they would wave to someone approaching them, wait for that person to join their group, then melt out of sight into the black heat.

Eunice stood looking at all this for a while, then moved over to the cabstand at the far end of the station. Several men were lounging in back of their cabs calling to anyone who passed, asking them if they needed a cab. Eunice went to an empty one. Presently the driver got in and started the motor. Greased flaps of hair slid back and forth across his forehead as the shiny caramel face turned and leered at her.

"Where you say you wants to go, babe?"

Eunice tightened, then relaxed. "Take me to a cheap hotel near the 3600 block on Bidwell Street. And drive down Bidwell Street."

"Yes'm. Sure thing. And can I come go with you?"

"Look here, you just carry me there safely. I'll give you your money and you can go on to your other business."

"Well, we could go get us a beer, it being so hot and all."

"Just take me to a hotel. I have no time for you."

"Yes, *ma'm*."

By this time they had passed through the downtown section of the city, Raleigh, and were bumping along unpaved streets crowded with ramshackle houses as close together as a mouthful of rotten teeth. Young children were running about screaming and jumping in the night. Men were ambling down the streets slowly swinging their hands about. Some were going out of or into pool halls and beer parlors, where loud music filled the rooms and slopped outside. It sometimes caught the men walking down the street, who would stop and shuffle out a dance step as they passed.

"Miss, we just done gone down Bidwell Street, and here a hotel. This all right?"

Eunice paid the driver, got her bag and guitar out. The cab drove off and she stood in front of the hotel. Above her a red neon sign flashed CALVERT HOTEL. She pushed open the door.

A bell jarred and out from the recess of the lobby came a pear-shaped woman with braids covering her conical head. Her bright black eyes surveyed Eunice. "Yeah?"

Eunice asked for the cheapest room and was directed up a staircase to the second floor, and from there to a room near the back.

"You gots a bath next door, and you gots a radio, and you gots a air conditioner, and I changes your sheet. You wants anything, you calls over the phone to me downstair, and I gets it for you. You pays in the morning."

Eunice slammed the door behind her. She set her guitar down and tossed the bag on the bed, then went over to the window and looked out. A rat scuttled along the sill, dropped to the ledge below her and disappeared, clicking its claws on the rotten ledge board. There was a house and a jook joint below, and music was rising through the heat. To Eunice the night seemed endless, as if it had always been heavy, hot, and black. She flopped on the bed and began tracing designs in the greasy dust-coated window; she could not think of any day in this place where the moments rode so slowly upon one another, exhausted before they came to the present. So she had come into this night to find her Orpheus, this man she did not know, who called her. Now was the first time she had even tried to consider what he could look like and what she would do when she approached him and said what she had to say; what she had come three thousand miles to say. Suddenly her hand dropped from the window and she wiped it on the bedspread. She had forgotten what she had come to say, and her image of him reeled in the corners of her eyes. The rattling air conditioner became a cacophony of discordant blues notes falling helter skelter around the room. A faceless figure, black and tight, wandered in front of her imagination. He was holding out a guitar, and from it was coming the music of the air conditioner. Eunice lay on the bed and tried to cohese the music into a face. A face was needed to tell him why she had come. But the notes fell and fell and made no pattern, made no beat, and still he stood there faceless, holding out the guitar. She jerked up and slammed off the air conditioner. The figure retreated into the fat heat and Eunice ran out of the room.

Old women and men were sitting on porches rocking and talking. Young men passed her, usually chuckling, "Hey, Sweets." and on each one she tried to fix a face for the man she was going to see. She crossed Bidwell Street, walked it until she found the number of the house, 3689, then walked back until she found a beer parlor. She went in, sat down, and ordered a beer. Behind her she could hear the clicking of balls on the pool tables, and men cursing and laughing as they took their shots. It was cool inside and the beer was refreshingly bitter. She drank it down and ordered another. She had not looked around, but kept her body hunched over the table and her eyes fixed on the beer can, but slowly now she shifted her eyes, and at the same moment felt someone moving toward her. She looked up and saw a rotten-toothed smile.

"Mind if I sits with you?"

Eunice said nothing, but nodded her head and returned to staring at the beer.

"You don't live 'round her, does you?"

"No, I just came to town on vacation."

"Now, why a girl like you come *here* on vacation? You must of got peoples here or something."

She looked at him. He had a pleasant full face, a child's face. She said, "Well, no, I don't have any relatives, I came to see a friend."

His smile dropped for a moment. "Oh, you don't be seeing this friend all the time, does you?"

She said no, and they sat for a while in silence. Suddenly, someone put a nickel in the jukebox and music flared up. Again, the man she was seeing approached her, and this time his face was that of the man sitting by her. He was strumming the guitar and singing a jazz tune with his rotten teeth in a grotesque grin. The music stopped, then started again. Some man was biting out a song about his woman across town bringing him food. Orpheus slipped in, this time beating a tune on the wood of the guitar, and his face, that of the taxicab driver, grinned at Eunice. She jumped. "What time is it?"

Her friend looked up at her and said softly, "'Bout ten-fifteen. Want to go? I knows a nice place where we can dance."

Eunice grimaced. "No, man. Look, do you know a man named Blacksnake Brown? I think he lives around here."

The man threw off his soft look. "Blacksnake Brown?" he said guardedly. "Yeah, I knows him. Everybody do. You be a friend of his?"

"Well, yes," Eunice lied. "He told me to come and see him tonight."

"I tells you what baby. I take you there in a while, but first let's go dance some."

Eunice gulped the last of her beer. "I'm going now."

"All right, I go with you," he said. They got up and walked out to Bidwell Street.

As they walked toward 3689, he tried to put his arm around her; Eunice frowned and walked ahead. She felt like running, for the faceless figure was dancing on the road in front of her, as if he, too, was high with expectation.

They reached the house and Eunice rang the doorbell. A small boy came to the door.

"Does Mr. Blacksnake Brown live her?" Eunice asked.

The child looked at her with big eyes. "Mmmmm."

"Is he at home now?"

"Mmmm," the child said, still wide-eyed.

"Can we come up to visit him?"

"Mmmm," the child said, and stood blocking the doorway.

Eunice opened the screen door. The child backed away. "Which room does he stay in?"

"Uuuuhmmm, upstair," the child muttered and pointed to a door.

"Harvey! Harvey! Boy, you get your little black ass back in here or I beat it off right now," a woman's voice screamed from somewhere in back, and the little boy ran off yelling.

Eunice walked up the stairs to the room. She tapped on the door. A voice called out from deep inside the room, "Yeah, come on in."

Eunice stepped back from the door and looked at her friend. The voice she heard was slowly rough and delicately brutal, like stones being rattled in a can of ribbon cane syrup.

"What you waiting on? Open the door," her friend whispered to her.

Eunice put her hand on the doorknob and turned it. They stepped into the glare of a naked electric bulb. The room was tawdry looking, and almost completely devoured by a massive sagging bed. Sprawled on the bed was a wrinkled man with a greasy stocking cap covering his hair. He had on only white underwear, and it made his black body too harsh to look at. He was extremely thin, his skin mere tissue paper stretched on a rack of bones; it looked as though if he dared to articulate a joint he would rip like a spiderweb. He opened his full lips to speak, and there sparkling in the light was a complete set of gilt teeth, and set directly in the middle of the two front gold caps was a small diamond.

"Hi, you all." He raised up a long arm as he called out.

All of Eunice's strength was being drawn out of her and into the sparkling diamond in his teeth. She broke into a sweat and sat on the floor. She desperately wanted to leave, to run and blot out the black sparkling thing lying on the bed in front of her, but she had no strength left. She merely rested on the floor staring at the diamond. Her friend looked at her and took a seat on the bed. He turned to the figure lying beside him."How is you, Blacksnake? This is Eunice Prideaux, say she come to see you."

The flesh of Blacksnake's lips parted again into a wide grin. He relocated the wisp of his body into a sitting position and extended a hand to Eunice, who only looked at the long fingers, not thinking to shake it. He withdrew it. "Ain't you going to shake hands with old Blacksnake? Well, all right, you peoples is all the same. What you want, girl?"

Eunice was still gaping in terror at the figure before her. Now the lips, the stocking cap, the gold, and the diamond converged into her Orpheus. At last she forced words.

"Yes, pleased to meet you. Can I see your guitar?"

He flashed his eyes at her with a hooded dead look, seeming to sense alienation. "It be over in the corner."

She went over to the guitar and examined it. This was the instrument that became a part of him, this man who was supposed to drive everything to become the music he played. This was the guitar that the man heralded the sun with, this man borne by that same sun and decayed by it; this Orpheus with a diamond in his teeth.

"I axed you what you wants, girl."

Eunice felt tears welling. "I, uh, said it was nice to meet you.... I've heard so much about you.... I have lots of things to do.... I have to go.... Yes, it was nice to meet you... you know.... I just moved into the Calvert Hotel... and I've got to unpack my things.... Good-bye." She got up and stumbled out of the room, shuddering and cursing herself.

She heard a voice behind her. "Wait." It was her friend. "What the matter? If you really did come all this way to see him, why doesn't you stay awhile?"

"Oh, shit!" was all Eunice said.

"I thought you knowed him. You acted like you ain't never seed him before in your life while you was in there."

"Shit, no. I never have seen him before, and don't want to see him again."

They walked back to the bar, had a beer, and then went to Eunice's hotel. She walked up the stairs to her room. Her friend followed, but she did not seem to notice his presence. She went into the room, flipped on the light switch, grabbed her guitar, and sagged on the bed. She looked up as if she suddenly realized his presence.

"What the hell are you doing here?"

He sat next to her on the bed. "Sweets, you ain't even axed my name. Don't you care none?" He smiled and moved closer to her.

Eunice struck a chord on the guitar and said wearily, "No, it doesn't matter what your name is. I don't care."

"My name is Artis. What the matter? You was so happy just a while ago, and now you acts like you don't like me no more."

"Oh no, you're fine, but I'm kind of tired right now. I want to go to sleep to forget everything."

"Well, baby, let me help you forget," Artis whispered as he took the guitar from her hands.

"Oh, hell, I can't be bothered with you."

"What you say, honey?"

She could feel his breath next to her ear, and his tongue delineating its structure as his hands were doing to her breasts.

"I said get away from me!"

"Now, look here just one minute, woman. I's just trying to help you forget. Ain't that why you let me come here, so we can both forget everything with my special job?" He got up, turned off the light, and resumed his ministrations. A light flashed brighter and brighter out of the dark, a diamond light that blinded Eunice.

She tried to move away from the apologizing hands blinding her body, and from the infernal diamond light blinding her mind, but it was no use. Neither would stop. The more Artis fought to help her forget, the more she remembered the final face of the man she had just left, and finally she gave in to both, lying dead and letting herself be driven to a recognition of each. She waited until both wasted themselves on her, then got up and shook the limp form next to her. "Get up, God-damn it, get up!"

"What, after all I just done for you, you kicking me out?"

Eunice experienced a resurgence of strength. "Listen, you black, rotten-toothed son of a bitch, get out of this room! Don't say anything because I don't even want to hear your voice again." She was not talking to Artis, but to diamond-toothed Blacksnake, who was haunting her memory.

She got up, grabbed Artis by his shirt, hoisted him to his feet, and shoved him out of the door. She waited a moment until she heard him stumbling down the stairs, then went back to the bed and closed her eyes. Again, the air conditioner rattled out blues, but she did not try to gather it into any pattern. Under the music she heard the Orphic voice saying, "What you want girl?" bassing the music and giving it fullness. She laughed loudly to drown out the voice, but it continued in its demand, turning over and over in her being and keeping her from sleep.

two

The bed was soft, and Eunice was tired—of doing nothing all day in this desolate place. She had left her room in the early morning when the sun was forcing shadows down over the east side of the street. The jagged shadows from the uneven build-ings marked the area where the people gathered to sit and jive the day away. Only men were standing about—some clustered around a bus stop, some in front of a shine stand, some blocking the doorway of a pool hall—most with yesterday's clothes on, wrinkled, stained, and sour. All were old, not in age, but they gave the appearance of being timeless, killed by the constant plague of the sun. They acted as if they possessed some great secret that had died with them, and anyone who was not yet dead, who had not yet died in the sun, did not

belong in this place. It was meant solely for the dead and their
secrets, so Eunice walked the streets looking at the masked
faces, ashen even under the sweat, until they all looked the
same and she forgot about them.

The figure from the night before tickled her mind. She tried
to forget about that, too, but she remembered that she had
come here expressly to find this. There was no time for rejoic-
ing. There were no heroes here, only Orpheus, and Orpheus
was dead by the same sun that killed the rest. She looked into
the sun; it constricted the entire street, squeezing it dry and
leaving only the old dead men with their secret. She looked
into the sun, straight until her eyes watered and red streaks
shot infinitely horizontal to the sky from her eyes, and she
knew the secret. It was only that they had been killed by the
sun, yet must perpetuate a sham of existing. As the red streaks
faded, leaving shallow white caves in front of her eyes, she
knew further that the sham was integral to the process, a
surety that lasted, otherwise the secret of bleak self-knowledge
would also die. She looked into the sun again, the same one
that Blacksnake was supposed to have been borne by, but he
was a tired, dead man, a hideous remnant of some good-time
morning jive long ago, and she hated him for fooling her into
coming here. She hated him for his existence, and in the heat
of exasperation and fatigue as she walked the street she called
aloud, hoping for some respite. The sun only rose a bit higher
in the sky, the shadows retreated further, and Eunice ran back
to the hotel to pack her clothes and forget.

Eunice got to her room. It was cool. She called down to find
out when the next train left, but that was not until morning.
She lay down on the bed still cursing the black, diamond-
toothed man who, last night, by living, had damned her hopes
of deliverance. The bed was soft, and Eunice was tired. She
fell asleep cursing.

A telephone rang somewhere. Eunice woke with a start. It
was her phone. She picked up the receiver.

"Hello, Room 209, you has a caller in the lobby."

Still groggy with sleep, Eunice asked who it was. She did not know anyone in town except Artis.

"It some man calls hisself X. L. Millson. He say he speaking for a Mr. Blacksnake Brown."

"Mr. who?"

The voice repeated itself. "Just a moment. I'll be down. Tell him to wait."

It was dark outside. Eunice looked at her watch. It was twelve-thirty. She was half angered by being awakened, and half curious to discover what the visit from X. L. Millson was about. And though she resumed her cursing of Blacksnake, she dressed and went downstairs.

It was night now, and hot. The heat of the night was not the heat of the day; it was a penetrating heat, covering sins and bringing back life the day had pilfered. Eunice felt the difference and responded to it as she forgot the anger of the afternoon. She ran down the stairs to meet X. L. Millson and bumped into his belly at the bottom of the stairs. He took her by the arm without speaking and led her across the street.

"Where are we going?" Eunice asked.

X. L. smiled and said, "Blacksnake wants to seet you."

He led her down a dark alley to a red sedan parked at the very end. He opened the door and she saw Blacksnake sitting at the driver's wheel. He had on a red shirt, black pants, and a black cowboy hat. He was slouched in the seat alternately taking swigs from a whiskey bottle and wiping the sweat from his face.

"Hi, baby! How's you doing?"

Eunice sensed a strange warmth in his voice and manner that had not been there the night before. It astounded her and she almost forgot to reply to his greeting.

"What you been doing today?" he continued. "I wished I could of showed you the town, but I 'spect you got to see it plenty already. You didn't come to see me pick on the box tonight. We was all looking for you to come."

Eunice told him she hadn't known he was playing, answering laconically and hoping for him to talk again, so strange was his attitude.

"You knows why we is way out here in this alley, doesn't you?" he asked suddenly. "Well, honey, it's that I don't want to get arrested, you understands?"

Eunice looked at him, dumfounded. "Arrested! For what?"

"We-ell, you being fayed and all, I doesn't want to get in no trouble."

The night was warm and easy, and it came from Eunice as easy as the night. "Man, I'm not fayed."

He straightened up and squinted. "Well, what the hell. Is you jiving, woman, or what? You sure has me fooled if you isn't."

"You mean you dragged me out in the middle of the night into this alley just because you thought I was fayed? That's the damndest thing I've ever heard." But she knew it was not funny, neither for herself nor for him.

Blacksnake broke in on her thoughts. "Well, baby, if you says so, I believes you. But you sure doesn't look like it, and you doesn't even act like it, but you's OK with me if you really is what you says you is. Here, get youself a good taste on this bottle."

Eunice took the bottle and drank deeply, wiping her mouth with the back of her hand. They talked awhile and then she told him she had to go back to the hotel.

"All reet then. Listen, you come down to where I be playing tomorrow night. I be there looking for you. It called the Raleigh Palace Bar. In fact, you come in the afternoon. I be there early and X. L. and I's going to meet you there."

Eunice got out of the car and walked back to the hotel. She lay down and tried to sleep again, but it would not come. There was only the strangeness of the night deceiving her into staying to find out what the next night would bring, and she knew with happy despair that the next night would deceive her into an eternity of nights, waiting to see what each would bring. As for the days, she was positive. The days were of bare structure, barred by the sun. The day was a cage and the ones inside strained under the burden of perpetuating the sham, exposing their marrow.

Until this night she had been outside of the cage, but now she had joined them forever. The wizened jiving man had been the instrument by which she acknowledged her kinship to him and all those others who daily were squeezed into nonexistence, and nightly, in the ripe heat, violently asserted their being. His music was the music of such nights, the music of the evening resurrection of an entire people.

She had been looking for this night and knew that by her verbal ascension she could never return to her former mode of existence. She knew that now it was for her to jive, cry, and fall in the night, yet she did not know how, for she had not been born to it. Never had she been forced to her knees to beg for the continuation of her existence, nor fight both God and the devil ripping at her soul; never had she been forced to fight to move in the intricate web of scuffle; never had she been forced to fight a woman for the right to a man, nor fought out love with a man. She had never fought for existence; now she would have to.

The next day, Eunice moved to a room, knowing she had finally resigned herself to the commitment of waiting. Walking down the street she had noticed a sign on a café advertising rooms. She went in and located a plump man who appeared to be the proprietor. He was sitting on a stool behind the cafeterialike counter, and looked up at her with hazy black eyes couched in rolls of fat. He told her he had a room for six dollars a week. Eunice gave him the money. He led her around the back and across a vacant lot where some men were squatting about a fire barbecuing pieces of meat. They went through a path to a row of frame shacks. He handed her the key to one he designated as hers and rocked back toward the restaurant, stopping to kick a dog cowering near the barbecue pit.

Eunice opened the door and went in. She bumped her head on the sloping tar-paper ceiling and tripped over a broken chair in the doorway. She sat on the bed to get her bearings and something dropped on her head. She reached up to investigate and a gargantuan cockroach dropped onto her hand. She jumped up and stomped it, and as her eyes became accustomed to the dark she saw myriads of roaches skittering about the floor and the walls. She jumped to the middle of the bed, a board cracked, and the center of the bed dropped to the floor. She looked up to find the light and saw the cord dangling just above her, so she pulled it on and in an instant the roaches were gone.

Cautiously she stepped off the bed, kicking the dead insect under it, and went to the window. It was nailed over with a torn shade and when she extended the tear with her fingers she could see there was no pane. She went to the door. There was no interior lock and rags were stuffed into holes where termites had eaten away a good portion of the door. She turned around and saw another door. She went to it and it opened onto a passageway with three other doors. One was locked, the second opened onto a toilet that smelled of stale urine. A board led in from the hallway through the smelly stagnant water on the floor. The third door led to a kitchen that had its own distinct smell of stale bacon grease and greens. With growing disgust, Eunice was examining the cupboards and icebox when she heard footsteps approaching from behind. She wheeled and saw a round, glistening black man looking at her.

He took off his hat and bowed. "Is you the new young lady boarder? Well, my name be Shammy Thurmon. I lives in the room next to you. It sure nice to see such a fine young lady boarder and I hopes me and you becomes good friends."

Eunice introduced herself and then went back to her room
to unpack. Cockroaches ran at her footsteps. She locked the
outer door and unpacked her belongings. Then she sat down
on the bed and began to strum her guitar. She heard a knock
on the inner door and Shammy Thurmon bowed his way in, a
bottle of wine in one hand, his hat in the other.

"Well, young lady, I sees you plays guitar. That nice. I just
loves good music. Yes, Shammy Thurmon just love it. Will
you have a taste of wine with me? You knows I's an old man,
and I don't want you to be mad with me. I just wants to come
and sit and listen to you play. I hopes you won't be mad with
me."

"No," Eunice said, "I'm not going to be mad."

"Good! You knows I reads the Bible, and, well, there be sixty-
six books, twenty-seven in the Old Testament and thirty-nine
in the New one. The first book in the New Testament is
Matthew, and he were the Apostle to Jesus Christ. What your
name?"

"Eunice."

"Yeah, mine be Shammy, Shammy Thurmon. That's me,
Sham, just like in the Bible. You knows I left here in forty-two.
It was me and two other black boys, one was name 'xactly like
me, Shammy, but the other, his name was different, it was
Wallace. Yes, all us black boys went to Maryland, and there
we went in the boot camp and they learned us how to salute.
Yes, Lord, they did. And then we went to San Pedro, way out
in California, and the next day they put us on them ships and
we went to battling, and you knows I done had two ships shot
out from under me, and I's still living. Yes, it were the Lord
what save me. You knows what they says—if the Lord Jesus be
on your side it ain't nothing and no one can do you harm. And
didn't one of us get kill. Oh, I seed all them white fellows get
kill, but not *one* of us black boys, and it were the Lord what
done that."

Eunice began polishing the guitar. Shammy watched her a

moment, then continued, "You knows there be five points of meeting 'twixt two peoples. Number one be foot to foot, number two, knee to knee, number three, hip to hip, number four, shoulder to shoulder, and number five, lip to lip. Yes, any place they say that be true. In Hebrew, in Indies. I was in the Indies. You know I gots me a nice wife, but she be going on in what they call the change. I knows you don't know nothing 'bout the change, but that be what she going through.

"You knows in the Bible, in Genesees, it was Adam and God, and God laid Adam down to the ground and plucked a rib right out of his side and made it to be Eve. And God say, 'Adam, Adam! This is wo-man, and she to be your *help meet.* That not mate, Adam, that *meet.*' I going to take up journalism someday. Well, you knows there was this tree out in the garden, and Adam and Eve went 'bout that tree just playing and dancing. Well, God came looking for them, and He call and call and Adam didn't come and answer. Then He call again and Adam came running to God. God say, 'Adam, where you been?' Adam, he just smile and was holding hisself. Adam say, 'God, I didn't come to you 'cause I were naked.' God look at Adam and say, 'Adam, how come you know you naked, 'specially when I ain't told you yet?' Adam, he don't say nothing. He just pull off a fig leaf and put 'round hisself and laugh. Then, *then* God knowed Adam had been jooking and jiving out there in that garden, and God say, 'Shame on you, Adam. You ought to knowed better!' What your name?"

"Eunice."

"Mine be Shammy, Shammy Thurmon. I knows you doesn't like me 'cause I's too black, but that don't matter. I likes you. I likes your pretty hair. Yes, Eve she was prettier than you but you do all right for me. Is you ever heared of that lonesome soldier? Yes, well, that be me. I doesn't want you to be mad or nothing, but you knows if I could just hold your hand for fifteen or twenty minutes, everything be all right. Yes, how you like to have a Black Daddy!? I knows I's black and ugly, but the Lord take such good care of me, so I don't like nobody to ridiclue me or ride me down. What you say your name be again?"

"Eunice."

"Mine be Shammy, and I likes to talk with you because you doesn't ridiclue me, and my wife be going through that change of life. You gots understanding, and the Lord give it to you. You knows I going to take up journalism, and one day, the good Lord willing, you be seeing me preach the Gospel of the good Lord Jesus, but I tells you, you so pretty and I wants to hold your hand for fifteen or twenty minutes every day and be a good Black Daddy to you. Well, does you want Shammy to be your Black Daddy and give you money and loving?"

"Not particularly."

"Well, that no matter. I's going to keep on trying and some old day you's going to come running to Shammy and be begging, and with the goodness out of my black heart, I's going to listen and take you in. That me, Shammy."

"Fine," Eunice said. "It's good to know you'll be waiting for me, but I'm afraid you'll be waiting a long time. Excuse me, but I'm going to play some guitar."

"Well, does you mind if Black Shammy Thurmon sets here a bit and listens to you?"

"No," Eunice said. She picked up the guitar and began to play.

"Lady, Mr. Shammy would highly appreciate it if you could play them 'Moons River'! I likes that."

"I don't know that one."

"Well, hows about the 'Rocksy Mountains,' does you know that?" Eunice began to play, and Shammy rocked up and down on the bed singing softly with her. "Oh, yeah! Play that again; I sure does love that song. It puts me in mind of them times when me and my black buddies was out West, we was on our way to them ships and we was going through them Rocksy Mountains. Well, looka here, I'm got to go down to the store and get us some more wine. I's coming back and you play some more of that song for me, and then maybe Shammy going to preach a bit for you."

He got up and bowed his way out of the room. Eunice bolted the door behind him, changed her clothes, and went out to find the Raleigh Palace Bar.

three

The music began by straining against itself, each note deceiving the other into existence. Blacksnake was seated at the front of the bar, hunched over his guitar. He stroked the box, argued with it, caressed it, beat it, then made a grand reconciliation. And the music kept on gathering intensity like the shaft of a tornado, and carried everyone down with it, down to their knees and crying for mercy as the blues spun around them. Driving them on, he whirled them to the same mind as himself and whatever he said, they became, as he beat them down with the blues.

Even the children, too young to come in, stopped dancing outside the door and he sang to them *I wish I was a baby resting in my mother's arms, I wish I was a baby resting in my mother's arms, then I would have no worry, I would not know right from wrong.*

Then instantly, and with a new sound, he spun them up and against the walls of his amen and spat them back in the middle of the now silent bar with one last cry to his easy rider.

Slapping his guitar, he broke into an easy boogie, laughing out: *Say, I got a key, shine like gold, womens tell me it satisfy their soul. I'm got to boogie, I'm got to boogie, I'm got to boogie just 'bout the break of day.*

He laughed on and jumped up and down, sometimes picking out the words on the strings, sometimes throwing the box in the air, catching it and calling, "Boogie, *everybody!*"

Eunice sat, not moving, being carried along by the waves of jive and bodies moving in dance. Someone came over to her and sat down. She looked up. It was X. L.

"Having yourself a good time, baby?"

Eunice did not want to have to answer; talk would break the straining tendon of blues for her, but she said, "Yes, old Blacksnake can surely play that box."

"Yeah, you knows, honey, he been playing that same stuff since he been born. He done learned me 'bout everything I knows. We's tight partners."

And it came screaming through to Eunice again: *I got to boogie for my baby, every morning 'bout the break of day, got to boogie or Blacksnake just can't stay.*

"Can I get you some more beer?"

"Yes, X. L."

Got to boogie when I digs my gold, got to dig for my woman to satisfy her soul.

X. L. danced back. "Here you is, sweets—a boogie and a beer. You knows I likes everything about you."

The boogie ended. Blacksnake hunched himself over the guitar. *I got to, I got to find my baby, I declare that ain't no lie, I ain't had no real loving since she said good-bye.*

The music gathered momentum and people were calling, "Play that, play that, daddy!" Blacksnake doubled over the guitar, and every note ripped the air to shreds. *Yes, I bought that woman, I bought her a new pair of shoes, and she did not buy me nothing but the blues, but I just got to find my baby.*

Eunice looked up at X. L. "What was that you said, I'm sorry."

X. L. wiped the perspiration from his face and cleared his throat. "I said, baby, that I likes everything about you. Why don't we get together? I knows you was born with the blues, so was I and I likes that."

But I got to find my baby, yes, men, that ain't no lie, can't seem to find the poor child and I just don't know why.

"Yes, that's nice you were born with the blues, X. L."

"Well, now, I knows it is. And you's the one who be giving them to me."

Blacksnake raised his hand and called out solemnly to the moon. Eunice saw his face twisted and perspiring. Still, he and the guitar were one, moving and pleading. *Don't the moon look pretty, shining down through the trees, I see my woman coming, but she don't see me.*

"Whatsamatter, baby, don't you like what old X. L. says?"

I see my woman coming, but Lord, she do not see me.

"No, it's not that. It's just that I have somebody else on my mind."

"Well, now, you done come down here all alone. You isn't married, and you isn't engaged?"

"No, I'm just thinking about other things."

"What is that, now?"

"I told you, I've got somebody else on my mind."

Don't the moon look pretty, baby, just shining on down through them trees?

Eunice did not see X. L. anymore, she looked only at the twisting figure crying out *I see my baby coming, Lord have mercy, she do not see me. Yes, woman, you can cry, you can carry on all you want to, but that shining moon going to lead you right to Blacksnake's door.*

"Who is it, baby?" X. L. kept saying.

Yes, I can see my baby coming, but she do not see me.

"It's the Blacksnake," Eunice finally said as the blues rolled down and under her. The snake coiled and struck out again and again. *Don't the moon look pretty, baby?*

"Well, now, I could tell that. He strike once and you be dead, so watch out before you see his fangs. He just playing now, but you be ready to jump, 'cause he kill when he start to bite. He not young no more, but he done bit more womens than you can count on your fingers and toes. X. L. here ain't the poison kind. I don't bite, and besides, I's younger than he is."

Eunice looked at X. L. again. She wished she had not committed herself. "X. L., I didn't mean that. Something just made me say it. I'm not thinking about him, or anybody else."

"Ha, baby. You's been bit and doesn't even know it."

"No." But it kept slicing through the noise of the bar straight at her. *I see my baby coming, Lord, she do not see me.*

Eunice heard her name being called. She looked up to see Blacksnake beckoning her, so she went. He bent over her. "Look here, play a little tune on this box." He gave her a swig of his whiskey and wandered off in the crowd.

Eunice picked up the guitar and stared at it. She couldn't think of anything to do and people began to get impatient. "Get with it, baby," they were saying. "Hurry up, we wants music." She looked at them and started picking out a few notes, hoping desperately that something would come to her mind and fit into the music to take away the face of Blacksnake bending over. Suddenly it came out and she could not stop it; her fingers moved and her voice cried against her will, giving birth to the song.

Mmmm, blacksnake crawling 'round my room, mmmm, blacksnake crawling 'round my room, won't some sweet daddy come and get this blacksnake soon. And it flew on. *Mmmm, it must have been a bedbug, 'cause a chinch couldn't bite me that hard, it must have been a bedbug, 'cause a chinch couldn't bite me that hard, but somebody told me it was a blacksnake come in from the front yard.*

She quickly looked up to see where Blacksnake was, and he was standing behind her doubled over with laughter. Abruptly she stopped the song, slammed the guitar down and got up, but he clamped his hand on her shoulder and forced her back into the chair. "Lord have mercy, folks," he said, still laughing, "that done my heart good to hear my name called out in song. I wants this little girl to sing poor Blacksnake another!"

Eunice could see nothing but his diamond flashing, so she picked up the guitar and told him *You black and evil, you make me so mad, 'till I don't know what to do, I would go stand on the corner and find me somebody cripple and blind who wouldn't act to me like you do.*

He stood behind her with his hands on his hips. As he listened his smile turned to a hard grin and his eyes flashed fire. Eunice put down the guitar and walked outside. Behind her, the music followed, calling *Listen, baby, don't, please don't do me no wrong, I's just a little old blacksnake, and I don't mean no harm.*

It was hot and raining hard. Eunice walked down the street. Neon lights splattered up, undefining their messages in the rain. The street, haphazardly paved, was turned into a mudflow with people slipping and sliding down to shelter. Eunice skittered along, watching the neon fizzle and electrify the night; cars shot by, dividing the rain and mud, sending it rushing to drench anything in its path. Eunice, covered with mud and water, walked and was blind to everything around her.

Yes, they say when it's raining, that's the time a person have the blues, well, I can't help but have them 'cause my baby left me in my old run-down shoes. She was standing in front of a dark house. *Blues falling like showers of rain, and I can't even hear my baby call my name.* It was 3689 Bidwell. *My mother told me, don't forget to pray, I fell down on my knees and I forgot exactly what to say.*

There was no stability under her feet, just soft red mud clutching her there. Eunice bent to the ground and placed her hand on the mud. *Lord, I never loved but a thousand mens no way. I never loved but a thousand mens no way. But this rain have washed them all away.* She rammed her hand into the mud, bent down and pressed her cheek in it. *This rain have washed them all away.*

It was cool and yielding. As Eunice knelt in the mud she knew she had to get up, to go back to the Raleigh Palace Bar and to Blacksnake; go from one earth to another, from one body to another, but both were the same, both held the essence of destruction, of completeness—and the mud was so close.

The mud was cool, easy like sleep. She fell to the mud and lay there, sinking down and moaning to herself. Something was pulling her up. Something yanked her out of the mud by her collar. She wanted to stay, to sleep under Blacksnake's house until morning in the mud, but she was pulled to her feet.

"What in the Goddamn hell is you doing in the mud, woman? You's stone drunk." Eunice looked dully about. It was Blacksnake. "I been looking all over for you, you done left your pocketbook, and I figured you might be needing it, so I went to find you. But, shit, you out here laying under my window in the mud. You must be crazy."

Eunice wiped the mud and tears from her mouth and face. "Why don't you just kiss my ass and leave me alone!" she screamed, and fought to drop back to the ground.

Blacksnake grasped her forearm. "You is the craziest woman I done ever met. First you comes to my house all the way from cross the country, then you don't say nothing to me. Acts like some high-assed white woman, then tells me you is black, then calls me to be your man. Next you cusses me out, and now I finds you sleeping in the mud under my window. Shit! Goddamn it, if you isn't the strangest motherfucker, my name ain't the Blacksnake. I do thinks you is white, it ain't no black woman would dare act crazy like this, but it don't matter. You got to go back to your place and get clean up. Hop in the car and I carry you back."

Eunice pulled away from his grasp. *Yes, it must have been a bedbug, 'cause a chinch don't bite this hard, but I heard it was a blacksnake come in from my front yard.*

"Please," was all Eunice said as she ran off.

"All right there, miss! Hold it right there!"

Eunice stopped, completely bewildered. What did the police want with her at that time of night? "Yessir?"

They asked no questions, just cowed her into the back seat of the prowl car and drove to the police station.

Eunice protested and tried to explain, but they were busy with sending in calls to the station. In a few moments they pulled up to a tall naked cement building. Eunice was taken up an elevator and shoved into the booking room.

An officer at the desk said, "Godalmighty, where'd you fish this one from, the sewer?"

One of the officers who had brought her in stepped up. "We found her running around in the nigger section. One of them bucks probably beat her up when she asked for the money." He looked at Eunice. "If you got to get money that way, why can't you do it with your own people?" Then he said soberly, "Oh, well, I guess some like a black dick."

The other one said, "Hey, let's put her in with them, seeing as she's so happy to be around them. I hope the black monkeys tear you apart. You know, nigger women don't like you screwing their boys."

They took her down the hall and admitted her to a long

maze of red-barred cells. The jailer locked her in and left. His laugh was captured in the hollow steel structure and lingered for a long time.

Eunice sauntered down the walkway and made out two dusky faces beaming at her in the dim light; one was sitting on a wooden bench, the second was perched rather roguishly on a garbage can by a barred window at the extreme end of the long narrow cell. The one on the garbage can called, "Well, what they got you for?"

Eunice told her as she sat down on the bench next to the other woman, who suddenly turned to her and with the intense curiosity of an idiot examining a rubber ball, asked, "What izzz you doing in here, white gal?"

"Lord, Bertha," the one on the garbage can cackled, "do you think they'd slap her ass in here if she was white? You's nothing but a stupid black hefir. Girl, don't you pay that woman no mind, just relax."

"Well," drawled Bertha, "I thoughts she were white. She ain't looked black to me."

"Hush, nigger. You ain't got to *be* black to be black. You ain't got nothing but nappy hair and a nappy mind to go with it, old dumb-assed fool." She said to Eunice, "Honey, I's called Mozelle. Look here, you can share my cell with me. I's got the bottom bunk, you can have the top one."

She pointed to a dark hole in which Eunice could barely see two bunklike slabs of metal, a sink, and an open toilet. She got off the bench, climbed to the top bunk, and lay down. The women continued talking in the dim light as Eunice, exhausted, fell asleep.

four

Eunice woke slowly. Her joints were stiff, and she looked about in pain for her mother. She reached out to grab the pillow and banged against steel. Vaguely, she wondered about it and was slightly annoyed, then rolled over resignedly to wait for the alarm clock to ring, calling her to breakfast. She waited, and still it did not ring, and she turned over again, glad of the few minutes' respite. Then she groaned in her semi-comatose state and realized today was her cotillion.

Her mind fell back to the long days prefacing it: the instruction in the art of formal dance; the rounds of parties she had thought stupid; the shallow warmth of brown bony young bodies quickly met in dark moments; the inculcation of a breathless attitude in waiting for the moment of debut; the society women of eternal agelessness gathering for tea and talk.

It had been at one of those teas, when the photographers had come to make pictures for the local Negro newspaper, that she decided to leave. She mumbled in her sleep, remembering the women who had come dressed in all the grotesque finery at their disposal, and as fat as most of them were, they managed to sit like china dolls and chatter to the girls, seemingly unruffled by the beads of sweat that clustered above their lips, and the faint odor of sweat emanating from their armpits. She remembered how she had watched them talk as the classical music fingered through the room and the teacups clinked. She had not wanted to attend and invariably she would sit off to the side, gulping one cup of tea after another and affecting a cynical pose. At this meeting, though, she had become thoroughly disgusted and had slipped upstairs.

She went to the phonograph there and looked through the stack of records under it. Down at the bottom, dusty and scratched, she found an old 78 recording called "Bakershop Blues" by a man named Blacksnake Brown, accompanied by the Royal Sheiks. She lifted off the classical album, slipped on the 78, then turned the volume up. It started scratching its tune.

I want to know if your jelly roll's fresh, or is it stale, I want to know if your jelly roll's fresh, or is it stale? Well, woman, I'm going to buy me some jelly roll if I have got to go to jail.

Almost immediately she heard shouts and shrieks from the other room.

". . . Oh, yeah, get to it. . . . Laura, woman, how long since your husband's seen you jelly roll?"

"Gertrude, don't you ask me questions like that. Eh, how long since your husband's seen you?"

Eunice went back downstairs. Everyone had relaxed. Some women were unbuckling their stockings, others were loosening the belts around their waists. Someone had gotten out brandy and was pouring it into the teacups.

"Give some to the debs," someone said, "show them what this society really is."

Eunice sat down. The record ground on and on, and it was then that she knew that she had to go find the source of herself, this music that moved her and the others, however much they tried to deny it.

Something was bumping underneath her. She wondered why her mother would be fooling around under the bed, but she thought she was probably trying to find the white satin pumps to go with her cotillion dress. She raised up to tell her mother to go away, she wouldn't be there tonight, that she was going away, but as she was about to, she saw Mozelle's pink head scarf cross her line of vision.

"Get up, get up and wash yourself off. We got to go eat directly," Mozelle whispered.

Eunice jumped out of the bunk, found a basin at the back of the cell, filled it with water, and cleaned off. Mozelle gave her a fresh dress to put on, then Eunice went out of the barred partition to the garbage can by the window.

She climbed up, sat down on it, and looked outside. The streets below were deserted, save for a few delivery men trudging in the early-morning heat. *It's early in the morning, well, when I rise, Lordy, Mama. . . .* It was a deceit of tones that had brought her here, back to the "Bakershop Blues," and off in the distance, beyond the buildings, she could see a train cutting through the pine forest. *It's early in the morning, well, when I rise, Lordy, Mama. . . .* All she could hear was a low rumbling as it passed over the bayou bridge five or ten miles away, and there was nothing left to do but wait for the next train to clank by. *And I's got misery, Mama, in my right side.*

Something was rattling in the hall. Eunice swung around and saw trusties bringing in plates of food. She joined the others at the door and received her food—brains and eggs, and a cake of dry grits. She went back and sat on the garbage can. She picked at the food and turned to throw it out the window to the pigeons.

Bertha yanked it from her hand. "If you don't want that, let me have it."

Eunice let her have it, and turned back to watch the street below. Sound reached up to the cells in a faint jumble. When the meal was finished, the trusties brought in baskets of beans. Eunice sat down on the bench and took a handful of beans and a newspaper. She watched the others go about snapping them and did the same.

Eunice looked over at Mozelle. "Why are you here?"

Mozelle laughed. "Honey, I done killed old Latimore McDuff, and Bertha here ain't nothing but a old whiskey-headed nigger."

"Why did you?"

"Aw, I don't wants to go through with that no more, but since you ask, he just kept on bothering me and breaking in on me, so finally he bothered me so much I had to go shoot off his old cock-sucking face."

Bertha looked up. "Well, sho is, ain't he."

Mozelle turned around. "Shut up, you hefir. You don't know."

"Well, sho don't, does I."

Mozelle stopped snapping the beans and went to the window. She pressed her forehead against the bars. "I'm got to look for Ralphie this time of the morning."

The others went on with the work. Eunice's wrists ached from the bending back and forth and she watched cockroaches and worms wriggle out of the basket of beans.

Presently Mozelle began flapping her arms out of the bars,

yelling wildly, "Ralphie, hey, Ralphie! Go get me some cigarettes! Damn you, man. Can't you hear me calling you?" She pounded on the bars and began crying. "He is the dumbest man I done *ever* seen, didn't even look up here to see if I wants anything, and he knows I's here."

Bertha turned around. "Well, sho is, ain't he."

"Goddamn it, woman," Mozelle screamed, "I done told you to shut up. . . . Aw, shit, screw them beans, let's play some pitty pats." She went to her bed, took out a pack of cards from a canvas sack, and they began to play for what money they had.

Later on that afternoon the downstairs doors opened and another woman was brought up. She shuffled in the cell and lay down on a bench, moaning.

Mozelle went over to her. "Whatsamatter, you going to get out of here soon. Don't you worry none."

The woman drew her legs apart and her knees up. "I ain't going to get nowhere but over yonder." She turned away and moaned.

"Over yonder to the women's prison?"

"Naw," she whined, "yonder to them place in Virginia. Yonder there, they going to carry me."

Mozelle backed away. "Girl, why they going to put you in the 'tution? You crazy?"

The woman looked at her. "Naw, I ain't crazy. I likes to be there. Them peoples gives you new clothes and nice places to live and candy and cigarettes."

Mozelle eyed her suspiciously. "Why they carrying you there?"

"They going to help me get out the way of them haints. I done told them I'm got to get away."

Mozelle's eyes brightened and she sat by the woman's head. "Who was them haints what was hainting you?"

The woman sat up and put her hands in her lap. Her eyes

rolled. "People was 'tempting to get my childrens back to High Points. They tried and tried to get them. I thought they was my friends, but they wasn't."

"What was they, then?"

"Them peoples was working for my hu'ban'. He done left me and they was working to get my childrens to him. I thoughts they was nice, but they would tie me up and beat me. One time they went and put me in the woodshed. They put ropes all round about me and commenced to beating on me and that night they left me there and stealed my childrens. Old woman who was living in the back of me finally come and loosed me. I got me a pitchfork and went after them. I killed one when she was resting on her front porch. The marshal come and got me and carried me down there to Virginia, but whilst I was down there a haint commenced to hainting me. I went back to High Points to cross the water and get myself rid of them. Now the marshal come got me again and he fixing to carry me back down to Virginia. All I wants to do is go on back, else to High Points so I can kill the rest of them."

Mozelle snorted, left the moaning woman, and went back to her bunk. Suddenly the woman jumped up, made the sign of the cross backward three times, and started mumbling something unintelligible. Eunice moved toward her and stared. The woman began screaming. "Lord, Lord. Please help Ula. I done went 'cross the water. I done did everything, but since I's 'bout to go back, they's after me again. Help! Help! I wants to get out of here! *Out* of here!"

Mozelle yelled from her cell. "Shut up, woman, I's trying to sleep!"

The woman paled and shook. "Who that calling me from them walls? Ha, they gets you even in jail. Oh, Lord."

Mozelle called Eunice. "Come here, girl. We got to have us some fun with this old gal. You just watch what I's going to do." She got up and went to the woman. "Sweetie, what *is* your name?"

She looked at Mozelle. Her eyes were glazed and she was trembling. "I's called Ula Jenks. Ula Jenks."

Mozelle smiled. "Is you sure that be you?"

Ula looked up. "Sure, I's sure. I's me."

Mozelle gently placed her hand on Ula's shoulder. "You knows, Eunice, you recalls how I done told you that I went and killed old Latimore?"

"Yes."

"Well, one thing I didn't tell you. The night after I shot him I was laying up in the bed, them police hadn't come got me yet, and I was living easy. Well, nigh on to midnight I hears a noise by the window. I look up and there standing over my bed was old Latimore. He still had that hole in his gut where I had done shot him. I didn't know what to do. I turned to him and say, 'Scat, Latimore.' He look at me and as he leave, he say, 'Woman, you ain't going to get no peace of mind from now on.' " She smiled at Ula and patted her on the head. "You remembers, Bertha?"

"Oh, yeah, sho do, don't I."

Mozelle smiled at Ula again. "Miss Ula, now is you sure them haints can come after you even in the jailhouse?"

Ula quivered and looked around. "Well, they's got me sure enough."

"Well," Mozelle said, scrutinizing Ula. "Miss Ula, do you know you looks just like old Latimore, that man I done killed? Ha, is you sure you ain't him?"

Ula shrank against the bars. "What is you talking 'bout? I is Ula Jenks. I ain't no Latimore."

"Aw, hell, woman. I knows you's Latimore. You done stood over my bed and told me I ain't going to get no peace even in jail. I ought to know who I done killed."

Ula backed into a corner. "Get away from me, Lord, get away from me!"

"Eunice, don't you think that be old Latimore? I sure thinks you is the spitting image, and you must of done come to haunt me here in the jailhouse." She yanked Ula up and grabbed her hand. "Well, well, how *is* you, old Latimore? I's *so* glad to see you. Come on, tell me what heaven be like. You looking mighty fine for a dead man."

Ula, in panic, struggled to escape her grasp. "I done told you once, I's called Ula Jenks. I *ain't* nobody but me."

"Latimore, you know it ain't right for you to be down here, but I is happy to see your face again."

Ula looked up. "I ain't Latimore. If somebody do be haint-ing you, you got to go over some water, cross yourself three time backward, three time forward, say 'Jesus, Jesus, Jesus, save me' from what you want to be saved from, but it sure ain't me, naw. Now, you let go of my arm and leave me be!"

Still chuckling, Mozelle got her tin cup, filled it with water, placed it in front of Ula, and stepped over it. "Will that do, honey?"

Without waiting for an answer, she went into her cell and lay down to sleep.

Sunday, after breakfast, they sat around playing cards until about three in the afternoon, when the door below opened and a white woman climbed up the stairs to the door.

Mozelle grinned at Eunice and whispered, "Watch this, honey. This woman a fool and she funny, but we gots to listen, can't do nothing but."

Bertha's eyes twinkled. "Yeah, sho do, don't we."

"Hush up and sit down," Mozelle said and cuffed her.

The white woman took out a Bible and extended fleshy arms through the bars. "Ah am Mrs. Ginger St. Johns, sent from the Greater Mount Olive Baptist Church, and Ah am here to bring y'all some words of strength and guidance in your time of trial."

She began singing and Mozelle started to plait Bertha's short hair. Eunice lit a cigarette and got a reprimanding finger from

Mrs. St. Johns. "It is *evil* in the eyes of the Lord to partake of smoke and drink."

Mozelle turned to Eunice and whispered, "Is you got an extra one? Give it to me." Bertha searched the floor for butts which she dismembered and rerolled, using torn strips of newspaper.

The woman at the bars turned red. "Ah said it is *evil*, it is *evil* in the sight of the Lord to partake of smoke and drink. Y'all are wrongdoahs and are paying for your crimes, and still you continue, y'all continue to wallow in your repeated sins.

"About a year ago my little girl was playing with anothah little girl. Ah saw them playing and Ah asked the girl if she was a Christian. She told me no, and so Ah asked her what religion she was. She infoamed me she was a membah of a heathen, idol-worshiping religion, the name of which Ah won't mention to y'all. Well, Ah just went and took that little girl under mah wing, and now with time and with the grace of the Lord Jesus Chrust, that little girl is now a Christian and a good membah of our church.

"That is to be a lesson to y'all. Ginger St. Johns would most sincerely like to take y'all under her wing and convert you to the love of the Lord. He is the Shepherd. Yes, and we are His lambs. Ah know that some of His flock are backsliders. And Jesus, being the Good Shepherd that we all know Him to be, will go back and make a special trip to comfort and guide these wandering lambs. You people are the wandering lambs of the holy flock. Ah am sent as Jesus' special messenger to guide y'all back into the fold, since He cannot be here Himself. Now, please, don't y'all get Ginger St. Johns wrong. Jesus is *here!* Yes, y'all, He is here! But not in the flesh. He's here in the spirit, living in each and every one of us. He is here like a hidden light down in the depths of our souls. For y'all, the light has gone out, but Ah am here to rekindle that flame of the love of the Lord Jesus Chrust. . . ."

Eunice glanced up at the barred window. She could see clumps of dark clouds treading slowly across the sky. "Mozelle, it looks like rain."

"Yeah, it do," she whispered, "and it ain't nothing I loves better than to have me a good man on a rainy day."

". . . if y'all can be filled with the love of the Lord Jesus Chrust, Ah can tell y'all for sure that your time of incarceration will not be hard. Ah know it is a heavy cross for you to bear, but if you will only let Ginger St. Johns reach out to you and light up—*light up* that flame, y'all will be so warm and glow with the new holiness. . . ."

Mozelle looked around. "Say, Bertha, let's get old mister jailer to let Petie and that man you likes in after this old angel of the Lord go."

Bertha ran her tongue over her mossy teeth. "Yeah, sho."

". . . Yes, y'all must learn patience from Jesus and repent from *all* your wrongdoings if that light is to remain lit. Jesus died that the world—the *world* might be saved. Yes, we must learn to be humble and patient before the Lord."

Then she glanced out of the window and saw the rain. "Oh, mah goodness, it's raining and Ah have a new car. Ah just got to be on mah way. Good-bye, and y'all be patient in the Lord and he will help you to do right."

Mozelle nudged Bertha. "Fool, she gone now. Let's go wait for the jailer."

Later on in the afternoon one of the jailers came by to check up. He stood outside the bottom tier of cells and peered up. "How you gals doing?"

Mozelle was sitting regally on the garbage can. "Well, I 'poses we be all right, but you knows, mister jailer, we's kind of lonesome."

The jailer craned his neck. "That's too bad. But you won't be lonesome for long. The grand jury's coming around soon to inspect the facilities. And I want all your cells to look *clean*."

Mozelle crossed her legs and leaned back against the wall. "Well, mister jailer, I thinks it 'bout time me and Bertha had us a man."

"Y'all know I can't help you on that."

"Mister jailer, does you want them cells to get cleaned out time them grand juries come peeking their red necks in here?"

"Just a moment," he said and hurried up the circular stairs to the top tier of cells. "Come here, you gals. What do you mean?"

Mozelle and Bertha slowly walked up to the bars. "You going to get us some?"

He pushed his face to the bars. "Lookit, gals, y'all know I could lose my job for that."

"Well, it look to me like them grand juries going to see one hell of a shit-hole mess 'round this place. I 'spects you could lose your job for that, too. Ain't that right, mister jailer?"

The jailer pushed a strand of straw-colored hair from his florid face. "All right, who do you want?"

"I wants Petie," Mozelle said.

"Yeah, sho does," Bertha drawled, edging between Mozelle and the bars.

"Move on back, hefir." Mozelle pushed her away. "You can't have Petie, too. You gots to get yourself your own man."

"I wants Lester."

"All right, gals, I'll be back in a few minutes."

Mozelle turned around. "Hey, Eunice, anybody you wants?" Eunice shook her head and Mozelle shrugged. "OK, if you wants it that way."

She went back to her cell.

The door clanked again and the jailer came upstairs. He unlocked the door. "Come on, if y'all are going. The boys are downstairs. I'm coming back in fifteen minutes, so make it fast."

Mozelle and Bertha ran to the door and were let out. More doors clanked and then all was silent.

Eunice went over to the window and looked out. Suddenly, she heard Mozelle scream, "Bless my bad-luck soul! Petie, how *is* you, man? Man, why you don't bring the breakfast no more? I misses your face."

Ula shuffled down to Eunice, who was watching rain splatter on the desolate sidewalks below. "What going on? Where Mozelle?"

Without turning around Eunice said, "They're downstairs."

Ula moved up to face Eunice. Her high brow was furrowed. "How they get let out down there?"

Slowly Eunice turned her head and looked at Ula. "Have you been asleep or something?"

"Yeah, I been dreaming 'bout crossing the water."

"Oh. Well, they're down there with some men."

Ula jerked and her arms shot up in the air. "Lord, Lord. I wants to go down there, too!" She ran to the bars and shook them. "Help, *help!* Get me out of here! Let me go downstair! Help, *help!* Get me out of here, *help!*"

"Shut your mouth, nigger, you's disturbing us down here," Mozelle yelled.

Ula jumped back from the bars and began pacing the floor. Every five steps she stopped and her left buttock quivered. She moaned and sang and clutched herself between her legs. "Jesus, Jesus. *Nobody know the trouble I seen, nobody know the trouble I seen.* Lord have mercy! *Went in the room, I didn't stay long, looked at the bed and brother was dead.* Help, *help!* Let me out of here!" She sank down on the bench still clutching herself.

Oh, Lordy, trouble so hard, oh, Lordy, trouble so hard. She lunged at the bars again and shook them in a frenzy, her hip quivering uncontrollably. *Oh, Lordy, trouble so hard, oh, Lordy, trouble so hard.*

Eunice got up, and taking Ula by her arm, guided her to her bunk. She lay down sweating deeply and singing. Eunice covered her with the sack and went back to watch the rain.

The jailer returned in fifteen minutes and led Mozelle and Bertha back upstairs. He was smiling. "Now, I want this place to *shine!*"

Mozelle tugged at his hand. "You better believe it, mister jailer, it going to shine so you can see your face shining in the commode."

She turned to Bertha after the jailer left. "Well, girl, let's play some pitty pats."

five

The days weighed heavily on one another.

Hour after hour, day after day, Eunice would sit on the garbage can, looking out the window, trying to discern movement in the wasting of the day, and just as often the wasting of the night. Her bones, though, ached to move. She ached mostly to run and to contract her muscles until they cramped and she toppled from exhaustion. Her mind moved, but always in a convoluted path, returning to focus through the window, causing her to hit her thigh absently and cry *Be so glad when the sun goes down, I ain't all that sleepy, but I want to lie down.*

It did not matter whether she was in jail or out, the same pain was there, the same rasping lethargy. Only here incarceration was tangible, and that was the unbearable part—to be forced into the realization of what was, whether she wanted to or not. But soon she came to learn that it was easier here. Everything was decided. That gave her mind freedom to wander through intricate paths of frustration.

There was no lying down, for the track of the sun was always the same. It did not trick her into believing it would be any different outside, for she had assented to the fact of stagnancy when she decided to stay in Raleigh, and if she had to, again she would lie in the cool mud, and again and again until she could not rise from it anymore. So she waited her days and nights out, never really knowing why she was there, but somehow accepting it as she tracked the path of the sun from the jailhouse window.

Late one night they had been sitting around the floor of the cell talking and shooting a pair of makeshift dice, made by thoroughly saturating pieces of paper towels with spit, squaring them off, and marking dots with the char from burned matches. Just outside the cells the electric light was making it unbearably hot. Ula, as usual, was lying on her cot fanning and mumbling to herself. She rarely got up except to eat or to suck her thumb and twitch her buttock at the trusties when they came in. For once, Eunice was winning the money. She stepped into the bunk cell for a moment to drink some water and heard the lower doors being opened. Immediately she heard screaming and singing.

"*Bring it on home to me, oh, yeah, bring your sweet loving, bring it on home to me. Yeah, yeah, yeah, yeah. . . .* Yes, well, bring it on home to Jacqueline. Who upstairs? *Who* upstairs? Mozelle, is you up there? I done heared they gots you in jail. Is you here?"

Mozelle rushed to the bars. "Jacqueline! What the shit you

doing here? Yeah, you knowed I'm got to be here, ain't study-ing 'bout going nowhere else. What the hell happened?"

"Oh, baby, bring your sweet loving, bring it on home to me, me, me, me. . . . Yes, *Lord,* this is Jacque*line!"*

Mozelle screamed, "Woman, shut up. We all knows who you is, but why the hell is you here?"

"Yeah, *honey!* This is sweet Jacque*line!* Shit, Mozelle, you knows I just got back from seeing my mama and papa over to Monroe, and I's so happy. Yes, Lord! *Oh, if you ever change your mind, about leaving me behind, well, bring your sweet loving, bring it on home to Jacqueline!"*

"Jacqueline, if you so damn happy, how come you laugh your ass back into the jail? Woman, I bets you a drunken mess."

"Goddamn, it ain't me what's a mess. You musta been rot-ting up there with your old nappy head of hair and ain't got no hairdresser to treat it. That what come from killing a man."

Mozelle patted her neatly greased-down hair. "Naw, Jacque-line, my hair's fixed nice. It so good I just think 'bout it and it lay right down on my head smooth as cream."

"Woman, you better keep your mind on it all the time, 'cause if you doesn't it going to spring up so high and so strong it hit that jailhouse roof."

"You knows, Jacqueline, too bad you ain't up here. In the morning I sure could use some of your old steel wool to clean the commode out."

"Woman, my hair so pretty and nice you couldn't find nare a curl in it."

"Yeah, that 'cause all you got is nap. 'Fore I done got in here, I was down one day to the Salon de Beauté where you goes and May, that hairdresser, told me, 'Miss Mozelle, I's so glad to see somebody in here who have fine hair. Is you heared 'bout what that Jacqueline done the other day? That woman come in here wanting a wash and a press and a curl, and I'm got to be always obliging to my patrons, so first I got her and washed her hair. It took me the good part of two hours to scrape the grease out, then all of a sudden that hair rise up off her head like it was a angel and it commenced to scratch my face up. Yes, and then I done broke three washing brushes trying to get through to clean that tangle. I done put her under the dryer and went to my work and just as soon as I turn my back I done heared all this whizzing and crackling and sees all this smoke, and does you know, that hair on Jacqueline's head had done made the dryer to short-circuit? So then I gets out the hot comb, and you knows it got steel teeth? Well, working it through that kink, them teeth commenced to falling out like they was watermelon seeds, and it took me five solid-steel hot combs just to slick down the top layer. Finally, I tells her I thinks she would do well to go next door to the barber and get a conk.' "

"Well, Mozelle, when you went there didn't you get your hair trimmed?"

" 'Course, woman, you knows I gots to keep in style."

"Well, I went back after that and there was a sign on the door saying we's closed for spring cleaning. But inside I could see old May down to her knees scrubbing the floor, so I knocked on the door and she let me in. I says she must be having it hard, scrubbing the floor all by herself, without no ammonia or nothing. She say, 'Naw, it ain't hard. See, I done got some of old Mozelle's hair clippings and them things is so good and strong I just touch the floor with it and the floor shine. Yeah, there ain't nothing better for cleaning than Mozelle's wool.' "

"Hunh, and while you was standing there shooting off your mouth 'bout my good hair, your sweet man was off with another woman. In fact, he come to me one day and say, 'Mozelle, would you come go with me a bit? I just can't take laying up in the bed with Jacqueline no more. Every time I wants to run my fingers through her hair my hands get all sliced up and raw and they's so sore for days I can't do nothing.'"

"Bring it on home," Jacqueline said, and laughed. "You knowed I recalls now, a few days after you done killed old Latimore I was reading in the paper how the police had done tried to figure what kind of strange old bullets done made that man die. You done clipped off some of your hair and wadded it up and shot it through a gun barrel as bullets. It ain't no wonder the man died—that a might sight more powerful than gunpowder. You knows, you should of went and gave me some of them Natural Nappy Head Bullets when I went after my man. I could of just showed them to him and the bastard would have gone running. Aw, shit, Mozelle, I shouldn't of taken that damn gun nohow. Now we's both sitting up here scratching our nappy heads in jail and I ain't going to get out for a long time."

"Shit, girl, you know you going to get out."

"Naw, Mozelle, I just done come back from seeing my peoples over to Monroe and I been gone onto three weeks, because my mama done took sick. And you know I went back to my man and he was just as sweet as could be. Then, somebody done told me he had been co'ting some old *passe'n blanc*. I didn't say nothing until I kept on hearing it, then tonight I axed him and he just say, 'Well, baby, you knowed it ain't true.' But when he sayed that I knowed it to be true and it bad when you been with somebody that long to have them do you wrong like that. It hard to forget. Now I done broke my parole and they going to send me back yonder. *You know you stayed out late at night, and you know you don't do me right, but bring your sweet loving, bring it on home to me. . . ."*

Mozelle interrupted. "Woman, will you hush your fool mouth and tell me what you done done?"

Oh, baby, please, bring it on home to me.

Jacqueline started to cry. "Mozelle, I done got so drunk I went out and got myself a pistol, like I always does, and commenced to waving it in his face. You knows I ain't never going to do nothing with it, but—*Oh, baby, bring it on home to me*—the damn police done come to the joint just as I was scaring the pants off that mollytrotter, and they throwed me right back in this here jail. If I ever gets out of here, I ain't never going to take no gun no more. I's going to take that bastard's guitar and crack it over his fool head. But if I had of seed that *passe'n*, I sure as shit would have whipped her butt with it. Being with him so long and him doing me wrong, it so hard to forget."

Baby, bring your sweet loving, please bring it on home to me.

"Jacqueline, what you going to do now? It a damn mess, but you knowed you shouldn't of been drunk and took that gun."

"Mozelle," wailed Jacqueline, "I knowed it, Lord, I knowed it. But he had done hurt me to my heart so much I had to get drunk and when I drinks I just don't care no more. Lord, I shouldn't of did it, but it was *his* damn black fault."

"Well, sho is, ain't it," Bertha said to Eunice, who had been sitting on the bench during the conversation with her mouth agape.

Mozelle turned around. "Goddamn it, hefir woman. Can't you see this poor child be in a lot of trouble without you coming 'round with your fool mouth when you don't know a damn thing. Shut up, at least until she get better."

Mozelle continued to try and ask questions, but Jacqueline had lapsed back into singing and would not answer. Mozelle stepped back and arched her eyebrows. "Well, I 'pose she ain't going to say no more tonight. Take it easy, girl."

Mozelle got up and went to bed. Eunice lay down and closed her eyes. She wanted to go down below and take the weeping woman in her arms to tell her in the movement of the moment there is no love, for they were both bound to a man who did not belong to either of them, but Eunice fell asleep remembering Blacksnake's hand on her shoulder.

The next day Eunice awoke to Jacqueline rattling her cup and screaming to Mozelle. "Mozelle, Mozelle, I wants some breakfast! When they brings it in? Goddamn, my head hurt."

Mozelle went to the bars and extended her hand below. "Jacqueline, when they going to carry you back over yonder?"

"Shit, woman, I 'spects they do it today. You knows they don't be wasting no time getting my ass back there to finish my sentence."

"Well, Jacqueline, I 'spects you ain't going to get no breakfasts if they going to carry you back to the prison today. Looks like soon as I get my trial I might be seeing you down yonder."

"Aw, Lord, Mozelle," Jacqueline screamed up, "what the shit is I going to do? I can't go back there. It ain't no telling what that black husband of mine going to do now. And I wasn't but at almost the end of my parole time when I done this thing."

"Don't you worry your mind, Jacqueline. He ain't going to do too much—he too black."

"Damn, woman, how you knows? I say it ain't no telling what Snake going to do next. He might take it in his mind to go down to South Bay and see them peoples there."

"Well, I guesses you right, Jacqueline. But they ain't a thing you can do now."

"Yes, Lord, and ain't that the truth. That what hurt me so bad."

They continued talking and breakfast was brought up. A guard came into Jacqueline's cell. "You ain't getting your breakfast. We're going to take you back to the prison in a while, so get yourself ready. You know, now you've got to serve another year since you broke your parole."

"Yes, I knows, I knows all 'bout it, mister jailer. But can't I get a little something to eat 'fore they takes me?" Before she had finished talking he left and she scraped her cup along the bars. "Goddamn it! *Goddamn it!* I wants some food! Mozelle, if I could *ever* find that *passe'n,* I'd knock her mouth in so it rubbed her near-white ass for making me do them things which got me back in here. I don't like no woman messing with my man, but I *hates* a woman that white go to fooling with him. Goddamn it, I wants some food!"

"Jacqueline, if you keeps on talking like that, they ain't never going to let you out again."

During breakfast two marshals entered the cell block and removed Jacqueline. Ula watched with watery eyes and twitched her buttock at the marshals, who chuckled. Then she went over to Mozelle and put her hand on her thigh. "I sure wish it was me what was going."

Mozelle eyed her. "Oh, you does?"

"Yeah, I do," she said and moved her hand along Mozelle's thigh.

"Haaaaaah, sheeeeeit, get way from me, woman," Mozelle said and belched loudly. She, Eunice, and Bertha laughed as Ula ran back to her cell crying.

six

Eunice was let out early one morning. The guards had come in
around eight-thirty. As she walked out into the corridor they
told her, "You better be gone from here. Go back home where
you come from, girl, if you don't want any more trouble."

Eunice went straight over to the Raleigh Palace Bar. There
was nothing much different about freedom, save that she could
drink now and forget. It was still hot, but she could sense
winter coming as she walked down the street. The sky was
white and the sun, very far away, drove its lethargic shafts of
light only here and there, staining the broken sidewalk.

She walked into the Raleigh Palace Bar. It was empty except

for a few tired men about the bar, leaning like withered, trampled weeds at the edge of a field. A path of sun extended about three feet into the doorway on the cement floor and the empty tables and chairs gave the place the appearance of a long unused classroom. No one turned to her as she silently went to the bar, got beer, and went to one of the back tables to sit down.

Occasional shadows of passing cars blotted out the slowly shifting patches of sun on the cement. They crept forward, down and under the tables in the bar, but illuminated nothing outside of their own span. No one was talking; the sounds inside were of beer cans being set down, scraped in raising, and set down again as the sun slowly crept about the feet of the men at the bar exposing the frayed cuffs of their pants and their scuffed shoes.

Then it shifted, fell back on the spotted cement and probed into corners of the room where dust was matted and caked. One of the men at the bar shuffled through the sun to a pool table, racked up the balls, chalked his cue, and the dull clout of pool balls sounded out the softer noise of the beer cans.

There was no insistence here, either to speed things up or to slow them down. The cold wintering light marked its own time—the day—to expose what it would until it was forced outside by the equally encroaching shadow of the doorway. As the day wore on more men came in, by ones and by twos, each for a brief moment shuttling across the waning patch of sun and revealing his chapped ankles, distinguished only by the bare contrast of ash-gray ankle bone against brown skin. Their procedure was all the same: over to the bar, propping a chin on an outstretched palm, raising the chin to gesture with that hand to the waitress and receive the can, then ambling off to drink.

Someone finally turned on the jukebox. A small sliver of outside light was arcing toward it as it lit up, whirred, clicked, and dropped a record onto the turntable. Soon the outside light converged with the blue, green, and red lights emanating from the box. Sound bounced out. *Can I play with your poodle? Can I play with your poodle? I mean your little poodle dog.* The arc of light just barely reached the base of the jukebox, then it curved slightly and diminished into nothing. *Well, that old poodle have a long shaggy tail, I tried to buy him, but he wasn't for sale. Can I play with your poodle?*

Someone dropped another coin into the box while the record was still playing and the green SELECT sign jumped from the dark space between the greasy chromes. Still the tired insistence of the song pounded on with the ragtag guitar making the words loose their force. *Can I play with your poodle, can I play with your poodle?* The sun had now moved over to the window and was forking out a thin pattern of shifting light among the words RALEIGH PALACE BAR painted on the window. The tattered light came in and striated Eunice's face, forcing her to bend over the table to shield her eyes. Even though it was hot inside, she could feel the clear warmth on parts of her face.

I mean your little poodle dog.

A man from behind the bar approached Eunice. "Pardon me, ma'm. My name Pullum. Wasn't you 'round here a few weeks ago picking on the guitar?"

"Yes," Eunice answered as she took another sip of beer.

"Well, we needs another waitress 'round here and if you wants the job you can have it. You can also pick a little guitar for the customers some nights."

"I guess it sounds all right."

"OK, then. You starts Monday. Be here at eight if you wants the job."

There was no reason, now, not to stay. She had been bedeviled by a myth. She rather wished she had never thought of coming at all, but now that she acknowledged its existence she could never escape the glorious empty dissipation of this life. There was nothing else to do but wait and watch herself rot. By herself and to herself. The people she was joined with in the process of destruction could not provide aid; they were too busy viewing the disintegration of themselves in the sun.

More whirring, clicking, and another record dropped out and down and spun around. The mechanical arm whirred out and greedily, premeditatedly found its mark. More bowel-wrenching drumbeats. *Remember me, remember me, darling, wheresoonever you may be; begging you please ma'm, please ma'm, please ma'm remember me.* Eunice turned her head and the sun banded her hair, showing glints of deep red here and there. *I woke up this morning, heard the bad rooster crow; I thought about you, woman, and it hurt me so. But remember me, please ma'm remember me.* One tendril of light struck at the nape of her neck between the hair. It was warm, but soon passed on into the plodding shadows. *Begging you to please ma'm, please, please remember me.*

It was completely effortless, with the songs on the jukebox marking time and the clicking pool balls countersounding it all until the sounds merged into one, becoming inaudible. Eunice felt the ease, the lack of rigidity, and relaxed. She would learn to live cautiously and underhandedly so that she might survive. She would learn to wrangle her way on and on to meet each moment, forgetting herself in the next and predestroyed by the certainty of the one to come. Guitars would serve only as an accompaniment.

She smiled and tapped her fingers; at the same time the remnants of the jail tightness disappeared. She looked down at the floor and saw her foot moving in time with the music, which she was not aware of listening to, even though she had been mouthing the words. The sun had finally moved on down the street, leaving the place in the semidarkness of late afternoon. More coins clinked down, more drums and songs, and every once in a while she consciously dissembled a phrase of the song from the noise of the now busy bar.

Someone turned on the neon lights. They sputtered and finally remained on, making Eunice's pupils burn and contract sharply. She got up and stepped into the doorway. The sun was swiftly disappearing. She held out her hand, placed her thumb just below one eye, closed the other, and the sun appeared only a thumb's distance from the edge of the horizon. Quickly it slipped below even that.

Eunice stared into the voluptuous sun, moving so slowly all day, and now burning grandly orange, then red as it was licentiously being sucked below the line of trees at the edge of vision. Only a pink-and-orange glow remained of the wanton blaze, but her eyes seemed blinded by the last flare as she walked back to her seat. The entire bar was an incendiary red sphere with depths indicated by faint outlines of chairs and people, made a bit more concrete by her stumbling over them. She found the chair by feeling with her hands, sank down in it, and slowly the viscous ball split, revealing the bar again.

Have mercy, somebody been talking bad about me.

The jukebox was moaning again and the bar was very crowded now with people coming in after work cooling their heels and throats and jiving to the music. It was still easy and free, all sorts of voices being raised and lowered joining in with the pool balls and the lamenting jukebox with its *Now why they want to do me so bad, take God up in heaven to see.*

Behind her, two men were coaxing a woman. "Don't you flash no five out your palm at me, nigger," the woman snapped.

Why they want to do me so bad, take God up in heaven to see.

Dolefully the man replied, "Well, now, I just want you to know I gots plenty money. It's payday, you knows, and payday for me means I'm in mind to do a little bankrolling with you, baby. That is, me and my partner here."

The woman cackled shrilly, and somewhere in another part of the bar another laugh equaled hers in intensity, but not in sound. Eunice felt it. She turned around to see where it came from and saw Blacksnake near the door flashing his diamond-and-gold smile at a fat, long-haired Creole woman who was poured over her chair rather than sitting on it. His lank old frame snapped back and forth as he laughed, and his fresh process rippled. He reached over and pinched some of her backside that was flowing out of the chair. He slipped a paper bag out of his back pocket, crimped down the open end, unscrewed the cap, and handed the bag and the bottle inside to the woman. She threw her head back and swigged thirstily. He took a drink, laughed again, tweaked at her nipples, and moved on into the crowd.

Eunice tensed; the fact of his presence made the entire room and its contents bear down on her. She felt she had to move out instantly into the night, but to move through the solid mass would be to give in to it, to acknowledge his presence, and to press against that recognition for escape. She turned to the wall to be away, at least in sight, from the pressure, but she felt it all about her, probing in and out of the music that with its pleading and crying was honing his presence in every available point on her skin.

Sound became all important, the instrument of pressure describing everything, the buzzing and laughing with the incessant drumbeats and pool balls clinking; she put her hands over her ears. A five-dollar bill couched in a brown-veined palm crossed her line of vision. Eunice turned around swiftly. One of the men who had been at the table behind her was bending toward her now, belching sour beer.

"Get the *hell* out of here!" Eunice screamed.

"Well, now, you don't talk to me like that. I gots more where this come from. Yours just for the taking."

Eunice seethed. "Now, if you want to *give* me the money, just lay it on the table and leave. If not, I'm neither in the mood nor that hard up to waste my time with you."

The man jerked away, but the sour-beer odor remained. "Listen, I don't take that kind of shit from nobody. Besides, you ain't going to get no higher price from none of us here, honey. We just can't *afford* it."

Eunice said nothing and he continued, "So you thinks you is the queen, too. Well, ain't that the shits." He gestured to someone behind Eunice. "Hey, looka here at this woman. She think she the holy mama, come down here just for the money then act like she wouldn't touch it if it was hand to her with a glove on the end of a long-handle fish pole."

Long fingers clenched Eunice's shoulders. "Well, why don't you just go fish somewhere else then. This here woman ain't going no place with you, and she just 'tempting to tell you so."

The man stuffed the money into his pockets and left. The fingers were unconsciously digging into her shoulders. She couldn't turn around, but Eunice tilted her face backward and saw an upside-down Blacksnake grinning at her. He released his grip and grabbed a chair from an adjoining table.

"Woman, where you been? I thought you had done left old Blacksnake. The way you acted so crazy that night I figured you to be long gone somewhere else by now. You sure put my mind onto wondering."

Eunice didn't hear what he was saying. She was at once relieved at the disappearance of the other man and struck back into the intolerable pressure of Blacksnake's presence. She gulped down her beer. "What was that you said?"

"I said where you been for two long weeks? I thought you had done gone."

Eunice looked at an ash on the table and pulverized it with her fingernail. "I've been gone—I mean I've been in jail and I was just let out today."

"*You* been sent to jail? What you do?"

Eunice explained the circumstances, and the pressure exhausted itself as she talked on, but he was not listening. He seemed lost in the problem of keeping his whiskey-sipping out of the eye of the management.

"Waaal, that's right bad, honey. Yeah, too bad. But you's all right now, isn't you? I mean they didn't mistreat you or nothing in there?"

"No."

"Good! Then take you a little sip of this whiskey and I'm got to kiss you on the jaw when ain't nobody looking." He slapped her thigh. "Ha! I come to find out one morning, whiskey the best thing in this old world. I takes it to the movies with me when I goes and sees them monster pictures. But you knows, baby, once I drunk too much in the picture show and I was seeing them monsters crawling all the way home, and I had them nightmares, too. I tells you, they was all 'round about me and scaring me so I got to get up and take a little asperine. Lord have mercy, I ain't going to do that no more."

"You know, Snake, I saw your wife in jail. I mean I didn't see her, but she was there. She broke her parole."

He squirmed. "Aw, shit, that old gal belong in jail. I loves her, yes I does, but she got to go her own way. If she come back to me, all right. If she don't, that all right, too. Looka here, I'm got to go out on a little run, so I's going to go find X. L. and tell him to watch out for you till I comes back. You wait here for me."

X. L. came over to the table, breathing heavily, and tossing his bulk down in a chair. "Have mercy, baby. Where the *hell* you been? None of us never know when you be coming 'round, or what you be doing."

Eunice explained where she had been. He laughed into the cavern of people. "Well, you sure as shit is one of us now. Say, did you see old Jacqueline down there? I heared she was back in the jailhouse."

"Yes. I never saw her, she was downstairs. At first I didn't know who she was, but she kept on saying that she heard some bright girl was going around with her man and when she got out she was going to beat him to death with his guitar."

"Shit, she do it, too. It just a good thing she in jail or she be down here right now with a pistol. She wouldn't kill him, she just scare the living shit out of him and make him out to be such a fool in front of all them peoples that he go crawling home. It tickle the pants off me to watch her when she come after him 'cause he just run like a puppy dog."

As X. L. was saying this, Blacksnake came back and sat down. He jested with his eyes. "X. L., what you think? We got this here Miss Prideaux back with us. What we going to do with her? Both us gots so many womens worrying our minds I guesses we got to sell her, either or give her to somebody else."

"Oh, no. I take her on."

"Shit no, X. L. Yeah, all them womens is so fine and they worries my mind, but you knows . . ." He laughed and poked at her breasts. "I just might get sharp for Eunice here one of these nights, and if I do, I let you be my judge, I be having this woman wishing to her shoe soles she hadn't never met me. And if I was to put my mojo on her, shit, she be the craziest milk cow ever been hit."

Both men laughed and Blacksnake started humming a blues. Eunice was embarrassed and angry at their caterwauling, their wits steeled by whiskey. She heard Blacksnake sing to X. L. as they laughed *Well, I do believe little Eunice is a desperator, and I tell you, I believe it to be true. Yes, I do believe little Eunice is a desperator, and I know it true. She may be loving me deep in her heart, but her eyes tells me she planning to kill me for sure.*

X. L. retorted *Yes, the way she acting now, she ought to be put to shame, ought to be put to shame; she give you an evil* _look, love you to death, then do a high strut to tamp down your grave._

They laughed again and Blacksnake said, "You knows I thinks I'm got to toss her over my shoulder tonight." He smiled at her and took her hand. Eunice stiffened. "Whatsamatter, baby, ain't you coming with me?"

They got up and walked outside. The music was still blaring, but Eunice did not hear anything. Blindly she followed Blacksnake and X. L. to the car. They got in and drove to his house.

seven

Slowly they climbed the creaking stairs, went in, and sat down on the bed. X. L. squirmed a bit to adjust his bulk, but finally found a comfortable position and relaxed.

"Goddamn, X. L. I ain't never going to let you drive my car no more the way you carries on. I ain't never been so scared in my life, and all we done was drove five blocks."

"Oh, hell, nigger, I drives good. I ain't going to screw up that car of yours."

"Shit, all you do is lay to drive it, and when I gives you the chance you act like you ain't never been behind a driver's wheel before with all that screeching and weaving and carry-

ing on like a damn baboon. Man, I's so sick, I don't even want
to talk 'bout it no more. Eunice, why don't you pick out a little
tune on the box for me? Play that one 'bout being so glad
when the sun go down. I likes that."

Eunice sat on the bed and played. As she sang they talked.
She watched them, and sang, almost crying *Well, I come to
Raleigh 'cause I been told; well, I come to Raleigh 'cause I
been told, those Raleigh men got a sweet jelly roll. And I be so
glad when the sun go down, I ain't all that sleepy, but I want
to lie down.*

They laughed and drank some more.

*It takes rocks and gravel, rocks and gravel to make a solid
road. It take a good-looking woman to make a good-looking
whore. And I be so glad when the sun go down, I ain't all that
sleepy, but I want to lie down.*

X. L. looked at Blacksnake and chuckled. "Reckon it do, don't
it?"

"Shit, man, I don't care how they looks. I just care what they
can do."

"Hey, *shank!*"

She played some more; they drank and laughed. Finally
Snake got up. "X. L., I'm got to lay down a bit, so why don't
you tip on off? I see you in the morning."

X. L. got up and put on his hat. "You going to let me drive
your car home?"

"Shit, go 'head on. I ain't studying 'bout letting you drive my
car. I'll be seeing you in the morning."

"Well, I guess Eunice don't mind if you be doing a bit of
co'ting, does you?" He laughed and slapped her on the
shoulder.

Eunice looked blankly at him, beginning to feel dread at his
leaving and not knowing what to do when he was gone. "No, I
guess not."

"You *guesses* not! Well, Lord have mercy! I see you folks in
the morning."

Blacksnake leaned over to her. "In the morning, you got to pick my face, but kiss me good now, like my women's 'posed to do." Eunice kissed him. He sat back and laughed, his diamond glittering.

Then he got up and walked to the closet. And somehow, just then, she could see the proudness in his body. It terrified her. It was not a youthful proudness like hers—green and unknowing—it was a battered pride that almost unwillingly showed itself. It was the proudness of having weathered innumerable battles and uncountable years. It was the sinewy proudness of raw being, showing the stress grandly, not yielding, so instead of dissolution the fibers tightened around one another and the being moved as a whole. He seemed almost ashamed to let it show, for he moved slowly. But it was like a cat stalking its prey and when the moment came he would strike swiftly as a cat and then calmly return to the slow stalking of the sun with his music.

Eunice watched him as he moved across the room on tiptoe and bent from the shoulders. His movements were erratic and unplanned but sure, and the seemingly unimportant things, as when he wheeled and suddenly tossed something into the wastebasket, became deadly indications of the bitter force hidden in his frame.

She sat on the bed, fascinated, then got the guitar and without looking at him sang *You made like a railroad tie, so thin and straight; you walk like you walking on soft-boil eggs.* He stopped, laughed loudly, then resumed his movements as she continued *Yes, baby, you got teeth like a lighthouse out on the sea, and every time you smile, you shine your lights down on me.*

"Girl, you ought not to be picking on the box so much, it late." He sat next to her on the bed. "Looka here, I wants to see you lie down here."

Puzzled, Eunice looked at him. "You want to see me lie down?"

"Yeah, that right."

Eunice stretched out on the bed and folded her hands sepulchrally across her stomach. "There."

"Shit, woman." He laughed. "I don't mean I wants to *see* you lie down. I means for you go get in the bed."

He crept over to the light switch, turned it off, and for one last time the diamond flashed in the light. He climbed in the bed and it creaked as his body moved under the sheets.

"You cold, baby?"

Eunice said nothing. She looked at him through the darkness, fingering the sheet. Then she heard a noise outside. Some wildly sad music was hagging the dark. It was a plaintive but insistent old, old blues and seemed to tread softly in, lonesomely and apologetically intruding.

She felt a hand grope for hers. "I axed you if you was cold, baby. Can't you answer or something?"

"Where is that music coming from?"

"Aw, that only old X. L. setting out in my car and blowing on his harp."

The hand tightened on hers. "I didn't know he played harmonica."

"Yeah, the old sonofabitch, that all he do, and always late in the evening under my window. But I kind of likes it."

Eunice shivered and listened to the music as she remembered the first time she had gone down, late one night and drunk, in a rotting building stinking of other bodies so hastily used, some for the first time like her, some for the last, and some merely for another moment of relief from the boredom. She remembered how she had screamed in agony the name of the boy she now forgot, how she had left drunkenly running, vomiting and clutching her soiled dress. For three days she had not been able to sit without wincing at the sore memory between her legs, and her mind burned with shame. She had carefully washed the dress, then, just as carefully, ceremoniously burned it and condemned herself to celibacy—until, still in San Francisco, she decided to love this man.

She had stolen the "Bakershop Blues" record from the house of the cotillion party, and the day before the cotillion took it over to a friend's house. They had lain on the floor of the old Victorian house, drinking Liebfraumilch and reveling in the intricate weave of the demented music. Eunice, innocently drunk, stumbled to her feet waving the bottle in the air and solemnly declaimed, "I'm going to find him, whoever he is, because I—" She had fallen back to the floor and clutched her friend, laughing until the wine she had poured down her throat leaked out between her lips. They sat up, still giggling. Once more they toasted her ridiculous dream and by the next night she had gone.

"Here, slip in a little closer to me and stop that shivering. You be all right directly."

The diamond sparkled faintly for a moment and the harmonica kept up its pleading as deftly and precisely he manipulated her through various realms of consciousness, decapitating fear at the vein as he gently made her one with him. He had told her not to sing so much, yet he sang violently as he plucked the accompaniment from her pliable essence. Desisting and yielding like a properly drawn string, being was given and taken and given again. Raucously and inaudibly the blues spilled forth, whirled down and sprang up again, with only a creaking bed to hold the demands of their tension.

Eunice rolled over and rubbed her eyes. Light jutted in from the window near her head. It was early morning, but the heat was already rising. The sun pierced the window, magnifying itself in her pupils, reflecting again to the window and driving back into her eyes. Even when she closed them, the fierce light burned through the lids. She squinted her eye and focused on a telephone pole, which parted and joined again where the shaft of sun pierced the window, until it seemed that the point of junction of the pole was the trajectory, cutting down and splitting the image as it united it.

She was acutely conscious of herself this morning. She felt

removed from herself, as if she were holding her body in her hand, a ripe tomato, and she was immensely happy. The faint sound of people downstairs caught in Eunice's ears and she listened to the muffled clanking and clattering, and wondered what had brought her here to lie with somebody she did not know. Blacksnake mumbled and opened an eye.

"Woman, why you jump last night?"

Eunice thought and remembered that sometime last night he had flung an arm around her. She had wakened with a start at the pressure on her side, and forgetting where she was, had fallen out of the bed trying to escape the arm. She laughed. "I forgot who you were."

He rolled over and held her head under his chin. She could smell the sweat on his chest. "Well, little girl, just don't you ever forget who I is, and where you is." He kissed her eyes. "I means that."

Eunice looked up at him. "Who are you?"

"I tells you."

Eunice shifted her position and he ran his fingers through her hair as he talked.

"You axing me 'bout what I used to be doing. Hell, woman, I can't hardly 'member, that being so long ago. You best ax Mama. 'Course, she don't know herself, not being where I was, and she so old now she can't hardly recall nothing herself. My papa, I ain't got no 'membrance of. He went and left us when I was just a baby child. I was the oldest child, you know. All my brothers and sisters—well, there was ten of us, and we was all out working 'bout soon as we could walk. Always either in them fields, else working for them white peoples, and mostly they was quite kind to us. Mama, she took in washing, and sometime she went out and did the work. My sisters all helped her until one of them died one morning."

He reached for a cigarette. "Yeah, I does 'member when my baby sister died. That was Vassie, and she wasn't but 'bout seven then, and me, 'round ten. She caught herself some kind of disease, quick-dying, and one morning she didn't get out the bed. I says it be quick-dying, but it really wasn't. She had some kind of worms that was just a-running up and down inside of her. Mama took one of them worms to a woman who was 'posed to be able to tell what to do. That woman took a look at that thing, 'bout big as a grass snake, and she told Mama to feed Vassie some little bit of chocolate every day. Mama did that but it didn't seem to do no good, and anyway this morning Vassie was 'bout to get up—she had to get up early to go out with the wash—and she commenced to choking on one of them worms. 'Fore we got 'round to pulling it out the old gal just choked herself to death. We went then and wrapped her in the winding sheet and laid her out on the cooling board and buried her. There wasn't nare an undertaker in them days, you knows. It was soon after that when I up and left. Mama, I 'pose, was having a hard time with all them children and the papa dying, else leaving, but I always did try to do right by her and so did everyone else in the family. Even when I was gone, I kept Mama in mind. Later on she come here to Raleigh to live but I ain't seen none of the rest of the family for a long time.

"Yes, I left Mama when I was 'bout ten or 'leven years old. I set out to work in them 'bacco fields 'round about the country. Shit, one day I was out picking on the box and some man come up to me and tells me they's selling horses over to this place in Fayetteville. I flashed my ass over there, and having saved up some little change, I went and bought me the prettiest old horse in the county. She was one of them white horses, and I would dress up in them cowboy clothes and just prance all over the county, riding and twisting them reins and calling howdy-do to womens."

He drew on the cigarette and laughed softly. "Mmm, child, did I have them womens running 'round me when I would be up on that white horse. But finally one day I came to be losing at coon can and craps, and lost that horse straight out. So I

couldn't do nothing but go out and get myself married. I
wasn't nothing but fifteen then but I got to thinking it'd be a
good thing to do since 'bout everybody else was either married,
else they was co'ting. I had done had my fill of co'ting
womens—not now, mind you, but then. So I went out and got
myself married. She was called Clarissa Mae Tatum, but it
being 'fore the preacher, it was made to Brown. I didn't stay
with her but half a year. She was the craziest-ass nigger
woman I ever been 'round, didn't have no kind of good sense.
I'm put in mind of one day when I went out hunting. I came
and brought her a possum to cook, then I went 'round to my
friends to shoot a little craps. When I gets home, here lay the
possum on the table fried up just like it was chicken. I got so
mad I had to hit that fool for cutting up that possum and
frying it in flour. I means she was *stupid*. And every time I got
in the right mood to do a little boning, she get scared I be
going to hurt her. It took me near on to two weeks of being
married 'fore I could even get close to her; see, she didn't
never have no man before. Finally one night I says, 'Looka
here, we's husband and wife now, and you gots to do what I
says, so just open up them legs like a woman 'posed to do.'

"She scream and jump out the bed and commence to running down the road. I got so damn mad I took out after her
with nare a thing on but my undershorts, and them peoples
never did get finished laughing at us running and screaming
all up and down the road. Finally I got her and broke that
maidenhead and knocked a baby up there, but by that time
I had done been made such a fool of, I left.

"Yes, I just left one fine morning 'fore she woke up out the
bed and headed down to Mis'sippi for them cotton fields. I
knowed it was wrong of me to do that to poor Miss Clarissa,
but she had a mama somewhere abouts and I shouldn't never
have went and married her in the first place. Is you married?"

"No."

"Well, is you ever been engaged?"

"No."

"What the matter with you, girl? Well, I reckon you's scared, either or you gots plenty of sense." He extended his fingers to her face and turned it toward him. "I knows you loves some big and brassy famous bluesman—who be it? Jimmy Reed? Lowell Fulsom? Big Joe? Maybe it be Muddy Water or Louisiana Red?" He stopped and considered for a moment. "Oh, that right, you don't even be knowing them, or does you? Well, just don't you take up with none of them. I thoughts you might be a desperator, but I don't thinks so and it look like before you leaves here I'm got to throw over Jacqueline, my wife, and marry you. What you thinks 'bout that? But you better not fry no possum."

Blacksnake leaned over and kissed Eunice. "Does you know, one of my cousins went off, she had already been married to one man, and got married to another one both at the same time. I doesn't know how the hell she done it, and ain't nobody ever found out how she done it, 'cause she went and kill herself after that.

"*Mmm, little Eunice, where did you stay last night? You know your hair all messed up and you ain't talking right.* Well, I does know where you was last night. Ha, shit, but whilst you's with me, you just better not be gone too long from me *any time.* You's not to get out of my sight. I's afraid you might wander off to some man just like you wandered off to me. And God have mercy, if I lie I hopes Jesus will strike me dead, I'm *got to kill you if you ever does that. Yes, I don't want my woman walking the streets every day. I gots plenty money and I gots a place for her to stay.* Come on, baby, go call X. L. and see if he can't come over here so we can go someplace. I don't like to be staying in the house all day long in the summertime."

"I've got to go get my things."

"Where's they at? All right, we go there, directly."

He got up and stretched his long frame, his head rag bouncing as he crept to the closet to get his clothes out. Eunice got up and went down the hall to call X. L.

When X. L. knocked on the door, Eunice was in the kitchen

fixing breakfast. She followed him into the room. Blacksnake was sitting on the bed half-dressed with his head rag still flopping over his face. X. L. dragged a chair around to face Blacksnake and sat down.

"Well, look like you two been doing some good co'ting last night." He laughed. "Hey, Snake! Looka here, I got us a little taste."

"Shit, man, that good. Hand it over so I can get me a swallow. Hey, woman, you want some? Oh, no, that right. You got to get the breakfast. Fix some for X. L., too."

Eunice closed the door behind her and went to the kitchen to finish cooking the food. She went to the icebox and found a half-bottle of beer, poured a glass, gulped it down, and poured another. It was flat, but she finished off the bottle as she bent over the stove.

When she opened the door with breakfast, X. L. and Black-snake were sitting on the bed with the bottle almost gone. Blacksnake was laughing. "Have mercy, X. L., old man. What the hell you talking to me 'bout your woman and it being so good with her. Shit, man, you too wasted out to be doing them kind of things."

"Wait a minute, Snake," X. L. protested. "I tells you I ain't lying. It was so good that I had to sing."

"Hush, nigger. And just what was you singing, old man, that it could be that good?"

I was singing *You goes in and out the window, you goes in and out the window, you goes in and out the window, you goes in and out the door!*

"Whew, Lordy, is you some crazy bastard. You is a lying motherfucker. Hell, if any one of my womens could lie like you's doing, I'd be having her in the bed with me all the day long. Eunice, baby, bring this food over here."

"Now, looka here, Snake. Don't you call me no man what's too wasted. I's younger and in finer health than you is, and you better give me this little girl here, 'fore she wake up and find

you dead one morning. Wouldn't that be some tragic thing—
she waking up in the morning ready for a little boning, she roll
over and find you stone dead and no more good to her. Ha,
shit."

"Waaal, that all reet. I know she don't want to go no place
away from old Snake. I takes them young, I takes them old. I
takes any woman who bake good jelly roll. We bakes it good
together, ain't that right, baby? Have mercy, X. L., I tells you
this girl so young, her breasts is like sweetmilk, and Goddamn,
it *so* good. Too bad you can't get none, but she be my exclusive
property, and any man who so much as look at her with a high
eye, well, you wake up one morning on the other side of life."

They fell to eating their food, gulping it down hungrily.
When they had finished and Eunice cleared the dishes, Blacksnake stood up and scratched. "X. L., man, we got to go someplace today. I just took it in my mind to go fishing. You go put
my guitar in the car with my fish pole and wait for me. Get
you a pole, too, while you is at it. We meet you downstair."

X. L. picked up the guitar and went out. Eunice saw a glass
she had forgotten to take to the kitchen. She picked it up and
went to the door, but Blacksnake tipped up behind and en-
circled her.

"What say, baby, that me and you play a little of this in and
out the window whilst X. L. gets his fish pole?" And not
waiting for an answer, with his hand on her thigh, he drew her
down to the bed.

eight

The sky was glazed white Monday morning. Eunice dressed quickly. She went over to Snake and kissed him on the jaw. He stirred and opened an eye.

"Where you going so early?"

"I told you, I've got a job."

"Mmmm? Oh, yeah, well, give me another kiss on the jaw and I see you later."

She kissed him again and walked outside. As always, the men lined the sidewalks jiving about the trivialities of existence. Now she did not bother with them. She walked into the Raleigh Palace Bar and went to the back. It was musty and dark in the early morning. Pullum, fat and apologetic, came toward her with a broom.

"Good to see you done decided to come to work. Take this here broom and sweep the floor."

Eunice grasped the broom and began to hit at the dust in the room. It flew up and around her head, making her sweat and curse. Up and down, up and down the floor she went, agitating dust and spiders, but not getting rid of either. When she had finished, Eunice propped the broom in a corner and sat down at a table. Pullum came out with a fat woman in a green housedress.

"This the owner, Mrs. Mozique. Whatever she or me say, that go."

The woman sat down and looked at Eunice. Her champagne-colored wig was slightly askew and her eyeglasses smudged. "Yes," she screeched, "we needs another girl working here. We pays you twenty dollar a week, and if you needs a room we gots plenty upstair for ten dollar. If you takes it easy and do the work, you be all right." She got up and waddled out.

Pullum moved up and sat where Mrs. Mozique had been. He leaned over the table. "Yes, you knows we gots rooms upstair if you needs a place to stay."

"No, thanks, I already have a place."

"Naw, I bets our rooms is better. And listen here. Old lady Mozique only pay the girls twenty dollar, but she and me gots a good deal. If you and me could get to be good friends, I can get you the room here for eight dollar and I can fix it to get you paid twenty-two dollar a week. How 'bout it?"

Eunice's eyelids dropped. "Well, I'll have to think about it."

"Don't think too long. If you don't want the room, I's got to rent it on out to somebody else. But most of our girls working stay upstair. Come on, you gots to wipe off them tables 'fore the peoples commence to come in."

Eunice got a rag and wiped the tables off. Another girl had

come in and began putting ashtrays out. She walked toward Eunice. "Hi. You's Eunice, the new girl?"

Eunice stopped working. "Yes."

"I's Christmas. I be working in the morning with you. Another girl, Johnnie, come on at five. Is you going to be staying upstair with us?"

"No."

Christmas opened her eyes. "You means you working here and not staying upstair?"

"Yes, I've already got a place."

"Oh, well," she said and moved back to work.

Presently a few men in striped work overalls and plumbers' caps came in. "Lord, looka here. What we gots now?" one of them said as Eunice asked them what they wanted.

"God dog, girl," said another, "is you working here now? Well, I'm just got to come in more often. Hey, Red, get yourself a beer, too. I wants to talk to you!"

Eunice got the beer and brought it to their table. "I can't sit down now. I've got to work."

"That all right, Eunice. You just set and drink with the mens." The high-pitched voice screeched behind her. Eunice turned around and Mrs. Mozique was standing in the doorway, her arms akimbo. Eunice sat down and the men began to talk to her.

"Here, Red," one of them said, "take this nickel and play us some music."

Eunice went to the jukebox, selected a tune, and sat down. *Well, I'm a stranger here, baby, and I just blowed in your town. Well, I'm a stranger here, baby, and I just blowed in your town and just because I'm a stranger here, seem like everybody want to dog me around.* The guitar screamed behind the voice and the men with Eunice smiled like silly boys and drank more beer. *Well, I'm going back home, baby, where I'm better known.*

"Where you from, Red?" one of them asked Eunice.

Well, I'm going back home, baby, where I'm better known.
"San Francisco."

"God dog, Red. You come a long way."

'Cause it seem like everybody here want to dog me around.
"Hey, Mozique, let me give you five dollar and take this girl off work for today."

Yes, I'm a stranger here, baby, and I just blowed in your town.
"No," Eunice said. "I can't, I've got to work."

Mrs. Mozique's eyes sparkled. She waddled up to Eunice, cackling with laughter, and put her hand on Eunice's shoulder. "Go 'head on if you wants to, girl."

Yes, I'm a stranger here, baby, and I just blowed in your town. It seem like just nobody don't give a darn.

Mrs. Mozique laughed again. "Ha, well, mens, I 'pose the poor girl want to work. Better let her for now."

Eunice got up and walked away. More men came in; she served them, then went to the kitchen to help Christmas prepare food. They worked over the hot old stove fixing the pig feet, turnips, and cornbread.

Christmas turned to Eunice and shoved a bunch of turnips in her hands. "Get these washed and then go make some hot-water cornbread. We ain't got no hot-water faucet so you got to heat it on the stove."

She handed Eunice a pair of pliers to turn on the burners. As Eunice worked, grease and sweat filled the room. Her arms ached as she cleaned and cut turnips, and lifted pans, wondering if Blacksnake had got up yet.

The morning wore on. More people came in the bar and Eunice went from the kitchen to the other room carrying beer and removing bottles. Most of the people were playing dominoes. A few were shooting pool and playing cards. As she carried the beer in, bits of stringent conversation forked erratically through the room rifling her temples of their throb.

"I'm going to get me a new crop of high-powered womens for the next twenty-five years. . . . Aha, haba, booop! . . . What you say you got, Eva Lou? . . . Shit, tonked out, baby. . . . Woa Lordy, put down that Goddamn big five if you *going* to do it. . . . Hey, nigger . . . Eva Lou, is you really got two nipples on one titty? . . . Goddamn, put your money on the table. . . . *Well, I knows you just a little girl, darling, but you old enough to understand.* . . . Hey, Joe, come on in. . . . Eva Lou, let me see that . . . *Yes, I know you just a little girl, darling, but you old enough to understand.* . . . Don't call me 'hey, nigger,' call me mister, Goddamn it. . . . What that, wine? I don't want no water. . . . Damn it, man, I'm got to cut your throat, you big black-assed mammy-fucking polecat. . . . If you got a dollar, I put your clothes on. . . . I's sure got to boogie. . . . *Yes, you old enough to know, you losing youself a good man.* . . . All right. Hey *Mister* nigger . . . Looka here, Eva Lou, she *have* got two nipples on one titty. . . . Give me that damn dollar. . . . Woman, what you doing here with that broke bastard? . . . Aha, ha ha, booop! . . . I got you out, and if I have to come down here, you can do it for yourself next time. . . . Shit, domino! . . . Mister nigger, hey . . . I's big as a bear, black as a crow, and talk more than a Goddamn radio. . . . Eva Lou, come on. . . ."

Eunice walked back and forth with the beer and food, sweating and her arms aching. Mrs. Mozique called her aside. "Eunice, you isn't being friendly enough with the customers. We gots a business to keep up, you knows."

"I'm doing my work."

"Yeah, I realizes that, but you gots to jive with the mens a little bit. You gots to do what they says. Looka there, old Potts just come in. Why don't you go over there and get him to get you a beer." She pushed Eunice forward and went off cackling to shoot some pool.

The man that sat down was very dark with a rounded

squashlike face. He had deep folds around liquid red eyes, and small lips with a protrusion in the middle that continually contracted as he talked.

"Can I help you, sir?" Eunice asked.

"Yeah," he barked, "get me a cup." Eunice did so, then went back to serving the others, smiling at their taunts but not stopping to answer. She was thoroughly tired and disgusted with their words.

"Girl," Eunice looked around to see Mr. Potts beckoning her. "Girl, come here." Eunice saw Mrs. Mozique smiling at her so she went over.

"Yes?"

"Girl," he growled, "take a taste of this." He poured her some whiskey in a cup. "It Wild Turkey, the strongest and the best. I buys only the best, yeah." He poured her more. "Drink that down and come on, let's go to your room, Red."

"I don't stay here." Eunice choked on the whiskey.

He seemed not to hear. "Well, I'll *say*. You sure is a pretty little thing, let's go."

"I told you, I don't stay here."

"What! You doesn't stay upstair?" The lines around his eyes swelled and bunched. "You works here, doesn't you?"

"Yes."

"Goddamn! What old lady Mozique up to?" He bellowed, snorted, and took a drink of Wild Turkey. His black fist slammed down on the table. "Shit! What the matter? We can go upstair anyway."

Eunice looked around. Her head was reeling from the whiskey and her cheeks were hot. Mrs. Mozique was smiling and nodding. She stood up and braced herself on the table. "No, thank you, sir. I've got to get back to work."

The protrusion in the middle of Potts's upper lip squirmed. "Goddamn, Goddamn, you mean old lady Mozique got something this near to white around and we just 'posed to look at it?

Shit! My mama'd whip me if she was living for passing it up."
He stumbled to his feet. "I ain't coming back here no more."

Eunice ran to the kitchen. Christmas turned to her. "Girl, if
you don't watch your step you ain't going to last long 'round
here. Mozique and Pullum's pretty good bosses, but you got to
play it cool to stay 'round. Just let her think you's jiving and
jooking but don't give nobody the chance to play in too close
to you." Eunice sat down and held her head as Christmas went
on. "I means, you knows why old lady Mozique got you here?"

"No," Eunice answered. "Pullum hired me."

"Can't you see, girl?" Christmas brandished the knife she
was cutting with. "They's only got you here on account of your
color. It going to help their business. You just watch them two.
Pullum's Mrs. Mozique's old man and them two sure love their
little money. You works here long and you going to find out
pretty soon you be owing them more money than you ever
makes. That why we gots to stay upstair. They don't never
bother us about what we owes them and sometimes, if we's
slick, we can make a little pocket change to help out."

Eunice sat at the kitchen table for a few minutes watching
Christmas deftly hack turnips as she sang to herself, then she
got up and went back to serving beer. The Wild Turkey was
turning strongly sour in her stomach, and try as she might she
could not sit for long and listen to the wet-lipped men cajole
her. When her workday was over, she fled the confines of the
Palace Bar and walked down back streets to Blacksnake's
house.

The sky was still white and the sun hung precariously off-
center like a rotting orange on an outer limb. Children were
rolling tires up the street, their bare feet slapping the dirt,
innocent and free in the afternoon. Eunice let her limbs un-
fetter themselves and gave in to the sounds of the children
playing. But then she remembered Mrs. Mozique standing
behind her, softly laughing and prodding her, the newly ac-

quired commodity, and why she had been so readily taken in, and she remembered even further back to a time when she had also been taken. But then, it was no longer her place to judge, nor even to explain, only to describe and experience; yet still she had been too trained to exercise the critical sense to give it over to others, even in judging a memory.

One particular time she thought of. It had been summer, and to keep cool they had gathered on one boy's porch to trade trivial children's souvenirs—tops, shells, knives, cards. One boy had an empty shell cartridge he claimed was from the war.

The children gathered around him, asking where he had got it, each one fingering it, multiplying it by many thousands and thinking happily of bloody fields in unknown lands, wishing they had been there to propel the shell across steaming enemy lines. The boy told them his father had brought it back from the war.

A small towheaded boy removed himself from the group and laughed. "Ha, your father couldn't fight. They don't let niggers fight in wars."

The other boy grabbed his shell and screamed, "He did too fight! He was a colonel and fought the Japs!"

The children between the two backed off, the white children behind the towheaded boy, and the Negroes standing around the boy with the shell. Eunice stood behind the towheaded boy. They began pointing their fingers and chanting *In nineteen-forty-four, my father went to the war, he pulled the trigger and shot a nigger, and that was the end of the war.*

The other group tossed insults back. Mothers came and took their children home.

Eunice's mother dragged her off and sat her on the steps. She looked at Eunice with sad eyes and made her acknowledge the fact of her race in words heavy with the weight of centuries. Something inside Eunice curdled down to her esophagus. She bolted up on the rickety porch and began stamping her feet on the wooden planks, her face twisted with a hate she had not known before.

"Neee-gro!" she screamed. "Neee-gro!" She was crying as the word came out against her will. "Neee-gro! I am not *that!* I am not a nigger."

Her mother rushed to her, but Eunice ran around her down the steps, blinded by her tears and hating herself. She wandered up and down the streets not wanting to understand, looking for bottles to break, and she would smash them in a rage until the anger cooled, leaving only a dull point in the pit of her stomach that stayed with her for the rest of her life. Sometimes, even now, over ten years later, she would wake up in the middle of the night and think of the word with a hot remembrance that made her grind her teeth and try to hide herself from herself. But no matter what she did, the ulcerous fact remained and she could not stop judging, since it had been already judged for her.

And even before that she had been drawn to the forbidden dream of those outside the game, for they had been judged and did not care to concern themselves with questioning any stated validity in the postulates. Playing with friends, running up and down the crazily tilted San Francisco streets, they would often wander into the few alleys between houses or stores down by the shipyards. The alleys held a special fascination for them with their rows of trash cans full of liquor bottles and empty cans with the rancid remains of creamed corn and split-pea soup coagulated in hard drops on the outside. Once in a while they would find more interesting artifacts, glorious treasures of used medicine bottles, old shoes, twisted toothpaste and sterile lubricant tubes, empty lipstick cases and indescribable pieces of trash covered with sticky grime so scrofulous that they had to be saved.

But though her playmates spent hours collecting their spoils, Eunice would tire of the game and wander off investigating the huge storehouses. The old buildings were not of equal depth in back, nor were they joined to one another, and there were narrow dark passageways between the buildings. She would worm her way in and out of these, for they were usually empty, though occasionally as she would whip around a corner she would hear voices and would tiptoe up to watch two or three men crouched on the ground, each holding a sack of wine, and shooting dice. She would hide and watch them until the sun went down, marking their actions and words, then tramp home alone whispering to herself in a small voice thick with the sympathy of their wine, "Roll that big eight, sweet Daddy."

nine

She, the interloper, came to stay with him and learn his harsh ways. Some days when she was home, she, X. L., and Black-snake would go fishing, relaxing down by the banks of the Little River. Time and thought crisscrossed each other internally, silently, and the air was swollen with things unsaid, things hoped to be said, or things expected to be said. Only the flies buzzed over their heads waiting to settle on the catch of fish.

There was no real thought, only the vague aura of waiting lazily for something agreeable to be said or listened to or not listened to but merely heard, for talk was essential to the waiting which was the essence of this life. Sleep was superfluous because it cut short the wait with undeniable finality. However, though no one said much it was not a sharp ennui; it was pleasant and quite in keeping with the land, where everything only wanted to wait—for what, no one knew, or really cared. The day was at hand and it was to be taken with a soft hand, dismembered and sucked slowly, happily until another day revealed itself.

Sometimes though, there was in them the inability to take things in the way they should; they had vague hintings at their abulia and it was often Blacksnake who found himself dry. He would say to X. L., "Man, I just don't see why the blues come in my house every morning 'fore day."

X. L. would shake his head in sympathy. "Yeah, man, I knows. Onliest thing you can do is turn on your radio and let them waste away."

Blacksnake would carefully examine his shoes to see that every bit of the surface was shined to a hard gloss. "Man, but I wakes up in a sweat with tears all in my eyes and I just can't see why."

Eunice sat silently by, because she, too, was coming to know the ossification of judgment.

Blacksnake would grab a bottle of whiskey and violently rip off the cap, drinking with a vengeance. He'd look at X. L. "Yes, you take a man have the blues, he can't last very long."

X. L. smiled. "Can't say nothing to deny that, man."

"Yes, he wake up early in the morning all in a worry and he don't know what is going on."

"Shit, Snake, you *knows* you ain't got to tell me. Man, where them dice at?"

And so they would gamble to release the pitiful curiosity. The charts of disgust were of no use; moments were to be used, not listened to in their swiftly aging agony, and they had only themselves to answer to for the crimes of forgetfulness, and not the world. It was painful but easy to learn these ways to dispose the heart to the memory of things never to be experienced. Sitting, eating, drinking, loving—all were careless expressions of something gone long before, casual in their very intensity, outwardly justifying only themselves but binding the people involved to the true yet stale verbiage of mothers' warnings. Long afterward Eunice could distinctly retaste the unique flavor of a cigarette inhaled early in the morning when she and Blacksnake lay silently in each other's arms, unconsciously hoping for the ascendancy of some sort of permanence, yet merely toying with how they would deliver this new day to themselves, scrape some sort of definite pronunciation from it. For already a portion of it had been lost to them by sleep.

That remembered taste served to refire the flavor of being one's own hostage. Everyone else was concerned with the plight of thunder, while they lay responsible not even to each other. Yet, he still heralded the sun. Not that it was a task of so great importance, but it was a signal of hated finality that he had been chosen to amend into life. It was a disgusting but necessary avulsion for Eunice from easily being concerned about things of no real consequence to her, for now there were too many things to say, and not enough words to express. A song and a touch were the only means to combat the harrowing lack of communication that became a faked and enforced privacy, making one scream: *Have you ever looked over a mountain, a mountain you have never seen; have you ever lay down in your bed and had one of those lonesome dreams?* And slowly she came to taste more of the marrow of what made blues than she had ever imagined to be contained in such a thin, rigid fiber of expression.

Often Blacksnake would lie down for a short nap in the afternoon and when Eunice was home she too would rest. She would stretch out, her head slightly below his, low enough to look up at him as he slept. Always she would see first the wrinkles at the base of his neck behind each ear that reminded her of accordion-folded paper fans. But these were soft and small, and converged in a rumple at the back of his earlobe. Her eyes would then wander across his ear, usually with her hands following, tracing and quietly hoping to remember the sensation of his face. She would trace the razor pocks on his cheek. At the jaw they were long and thin, like lizard tracks in the sand, but as they went up his cheek they became small pinpoints and finally disappeared with confusion under his eyes. Her hands would jump over to his temple, her fingers feeling its throb. His eyebrows were those of a small child, very fine and extremely delineated, and on his forehead she could barely discern the grooves that made the diastrophic contortions rendering his face unrecognizable when he was cursing or singing.

His skin was liquid chocolate, but under his eyes it deepened and dulled to a black velvet. Many times she would find his hands folded on his chest, take them in her own, and examine their weatherbeaten contour. The broken, distorted knuckles were the same black velvet and the veins knotted in and out, twining their way to invisibility at his wrists. His fingers were long, the tips calloused beyond feeling from pounding on the strings, and his nails ribbed and stained.

He would snore and sputter, sometimes chewing violently as if some tough hog hock was filling his mouth. Each time he would do this Eunice broke into laughter that woke him. His hand would fly up to check that his head rag was in place and his eyes would open. "Hey, woman," he would say, "what you laughing at?"

She would turn and try to stifle the laughter that rose in her every time she remembered the slow crackling of his teeth. "You were chewing in your sleep."

"I was having me a dream that my old lady was cooking me some food. She and you is the onliest peoples I lets fix my food, you knows. Somebody else might poison the Blacksnake. Shit, *you* just might."

"No, you know I would never do that."

"Yeah, I knows that, but, baby, I can't never be too sure." He would reach for a cigarette, so would Eunice. His hand would grab her arm and force it down. "Stop that. You going to kill youself smoking so much." Then she would put down the cigarette, get him some beer, and he would tell her stories as they drank.

"Yes, you knows, speaking 'bout killing peoples, one time I was living out to the country picking 'bacco. My wife was out there and she was Clarissa Mae then. She pick more 'bacco then them mens. I was a bad man then, and I used to take her money and go down to the town and gamble.

"In the camp I didn't pick no 'bacco. I let old Clarissa do that. I just used to play my guitar on Saturday nights and dance for them peoples. I was too slick for them when they would get to shooting the craps. I sure could roll them molly-trotters. I would get out there, set my point, and win all them store papers from them workers.

"It was them times when nobody couldn't get no liquor, so I'd go down and get me some malt syrup and sugar and some water and put it all in a crock churn during the week. Come Saturday night I play my box and sell the best-tasting beer you ever seen 'round Wake County, for thirty cent a bottle, and didn't no police ever get me for that."

He held up the beer to the light. "Shit, girl, it wasn't nothing like this. Then one time my brother came down from High Points to gamble. We all got to gambling and drinking my beer and he got to winning all the money. One of them mens got mad and left the game and my brother commenced to winning more money. Directly all the beer ran out and everybody got tired and wanted to go. My brother put all his little money away and just as soon as my brother gets out the screen door, this black fool what'd left earlier jumps out and stab him in his chest. My brother run down the street and he fell stone dead on the road. The other motherfucker hightailed his ass out of the country. I got so mad seeing my brother get kill for that little money, I got my gun. I used to had a fine old Colt pistol, shiny with a silver-and-mother-of-pearl handle. I got my gun and set out after that fool. I went and axed everybody if they'd seen him and I told them what he look like, 'cause he was a ugly fool. There was something wrong with his lip. He didn't have none, it just kept on running on up to his nose like somebody done hacked a passway right up his face. I was getting ready to hack one clear up from his black ass to his nappy head when somebody come and tell me where he be.

"As soon as I seed him I knowed who he was, and I just commenced to shooting. I *had* to kill his ass. His mama and papa come running and call the police on me. They carried me off to the penitench for five year. When I got out I went looking for the rest of his peoples, but they had gone to Chicago or someplace like that. I's sorry, sorry to my grave that I went to kill that fool. I don't want to be killing nobody. Now, I might just kill somebody accidental with my knife if I gets to fighting, but I don't be meaning to, and if I did they be sending me back to the penitench again."

He looked at his hands. "If I'm got to go back now, I knows, I *knows* I wouldn't never see the outside no more. I's too old for that shit." He looked at Eunice. "Yeah, woman, the prison blues is the baddest blues ever to fall down on this old daddy."

They would lie there in the receding light finishing the beer, telling lies and laughing, then listening quietly to their stomachs growl.

"Yeah, they sure do go on rumbling," Blacksnake would say.

Eunice would take a drink of beer, lie back, and laugh. "Well, it's not so much mine as yours."

He would pull the bottle of beer from her, take her hand,

and flash his diamond in her face. "You kind of likes old Blacksnake. He mean though, going 'round killing peoples."

"Well, now," she would say, still laughing, "yes."

"Why, baby?"

"I suppose it's because your stomach growls so loud."

"Shit, woman. That all? You trying to tell poor me it just my stomach that make you love me? You a jiving mollytrotter if I ever seen one." Then he would take her and pluck from her his special blues. And she would curse the joy of the song as she sang it with him in the dying afternoon.

ten

Time and understanding Eunice forgot as every day she had to rise and go to work at the Raleigh Palace Bar. Every morning at eight o'clock, she would be at the door, broom in hand, sweeping the floor, then dusting off the tables. When that was finished she would slowly wander into the kitchen to help Christmas prepare the food. With huge tarnished butcher knives they would chop, cut, and strip cabbages, turnips, carrots, pig ears, pig tails, pig feet, pig maws, neck bones, and chickens. With large stained wooden ladles they mixed meal and lard for cornbread, stirred pots of red beans and black-eyed peas. It was during these slow morning hours that Eunice was most conscious of a sense of captivity, not like that in jail, but of being trapped in a train of many hands moving with a deftness of despair from all eternity, never completely conscious, merely acting out what had been long prepared for them. Eunice looked at Christmas hacking at a head of cabbage. Her hands were black and raw.

"Christmas, why're you working here?"

Christmas put down the knife. "Aw, I don't know, girl. It 'bout the same all over. It could be worser, but I stays pretty tight with Mozique and Pullum, so it be a pretty good deal, I guesses."

"Yes, but how did you end up in this place?"

"My used-to-be old man worked here. I had done just come in from the country and he took me in. He was working here so Mrs. Mozique went and give me a job, too."

"Is he still here?"

Christmas went back to cutting cabbage. "Naw, me and him done broke up, and I was renting the room so I made him get out. I'm got to get out of here myself. I done seen some jobs open at the weaving factory. They pays more than here so I might go down there directly."

"Why don't you apply one afternoon then?"

"Girl, you doesn't know. I stays upstair, and old lady Mozique 'spects me to be up there waiting on the customers when I be finished down here. I can't hardly go no place unless I wants to get my ass whipped. I still doesn't understand how you can be working here and still not stay upstair."

"I don't know. All I know is that Pullum offered me the job and I took it."

"Somebody done told me you was staying with the Black-snake."

"Who told you that?"

"Shit, girl, I believes old Pullum know. If you is, you's a fool."

"Why do you say that?"

Christmas brandished the knife. "Does you know that man used to be Mrs. Mozique's old man? When she went and got rich with this place she quit him. He wasn't nothing but a damn sleeping-in-the-gutter wine-head Negro then. But I couldn't see that fat-assed mama jugging with his skinny self nohow."

Eunice laughed. "He must not have minded too much."

"Shit, girl, it must of been the funniest thing to see. 'Course, can you 'magine them two fat peoples, Pullum and Mrs. Mozique, huffing and puffing like two ground puppies caught in a mole hole? Jesus, but you knows that song by old Pink Anderson. He come by here one time and sing *Lean little woman can't draw my pay, lean little woman can't drive my blues away.*"

Eunice went over to the sink and drew water in a pan. She put some ammonia in, lit the gas on the stove, and set the water on to heat. Her eyes burned from the ammonia and she was exhausted already.

Christmas said, "Eunice, you best go 'head on in front and see if we gots any customers."

Eunice pushed aside the grease-spotted curtain and walked into the semidarkened interior of the bar. No one was there. She turned to go back, but just then a man walked in. His curly black hair was unkempt and little balls of white lint adhered here and there. He smiled at her like a Cheshire cat.

"Hi, Mama!"

"Hi. What can I do for you?"

"Is that all you can say to old Paul? Ain't you going to give me a good-morning kiss with my beer?"

"I'll give you a beer but no kiss."

"Well, that ain't no way to treat old Paul, because I loves womens. Get you a beer and come sit with me."

Eunice went back to the kitchen, dragging her feet. She knew another beer would make her want to sink to the floor and sleep; she had drunk five already, but she brought two beers back and sat down opposite him—it was part of the job.

"Well, that mighty nice of you to come have a beer with old Paul. You knows I is jicky, just plain jicky."

Eunice smiled tiredly. She had heard words like his so many times before, she could almost anticipate his thoughts. "Yes," she said with false enthusiasm, "I like to drink, too."

"Oh, you does? That sure is fine. Go get us another."

Eunice looked at his bottle and it was already empty, though she had no recollection of his even putting it to his mouth. She brought two more beers.

"Yes, girl." He laughed and slid back in his chair. "Has you got youself a man?"

"Yes."

He slid further down in the chair. "Is you married to him?"

"No."

Now his chin was level with the tabletop. "Well, look like old jicky Paul got a chance, eh? Is you got any childrens?"

"No."

"You isn't? Well, now, ain't that nice. I don't like to have no womens with childrens. They's too damn much trouble, always rifling your pockets and taking money, then telling you it for them damn childrens when you knows all they wants is some new clothes. Yeah, me and you going to get along good together."

Eunice arched an eyebrow. "Oh, we will?"

He pulled himself up in the chair. "Go get me more beer."

Eunice brought it and he slid back down. "Sure we going to, girl. I's going to carry you back home with me and show you to my mama."

"Shit."

He continued as if not interrupted. "Yeah, Mama going to like you. She done always told me not to mess with reds but I sees you is sweet." He lurched out of the chair and began shuffling about the table with the bottle of beer. It slipped from his hand and splattered on the floor. Eunice jumped up to get a rag, but he forced her back in the chair. "Don't matter none, naw, baby, let it lay there."

He began laughing as he danced. "Shit, lookit all that pretty beer done gone to waste. Well, I'm got me a taste of whiskey in my pocket, so that all right. Oooweee, child, you's so nice and soft."

He touched her arm. Eunice pulled it away from him. "Yes, Lord, you's so young and soft I be afraid to touch your titties, it might make jicky Paul want to cry. Oh, Jesus!" He began to sob as he tap-danced around the table. Eunice got up again and went toward the kitchen. He followed her. "Woman, where you going? Ha, you soft old thing."

He grabbed her arm and spun her back to the table. "Now, that better. Put you some money into the record machine and let's *dance!*" He reached in his pocket and change scattered on the floor.

"I've got to work."

"Girl, you can work for *me!*" He pushed her toward the kitchen. "Get me some more beer!"

Eunice trudged back to the kitchen, got the beer, and came back. "Here."

He started sobbing again. "Sweet thing, don't say 'Here' to *me*. You say, 'There be your beer, little bitty Paul,' then I says, 'Fine.' You says, 'Little bitty Paul, is I going to get my pay for that beer?' I says, 'Sure, honey,' and I leans over and kisses you like this."

He bent to her lips but missed, and Eunice felt the smack of cold, limp   wet lips on her neck. She moved away from him and he toppled over on the table, saliva running down his chin. "Damn, woman, you 'posed to *support* me. I's just a weak little man."

Eunice sat back down and laughed until tears ran from her

eyes. Still sprawled on the table, he propped his arm up, pulled down his sleeve, and thrust his wrist at Eunice. "What time it be? I can't see no more."

"A quarter to eleven."

"Well, Goddamn, peach-tree mama, your man got to go to work." He tried to lift himself from the table and both crashed to the floor. "Aw, *hell!*" He got up and stumbled out the door.

Eunice hurried to the back, got a mop and rags, and cleaned up the mess he had left. She went in the kitchen and dropped the soiled rags in the solution boiling on the stove.

"Christmas, I'm exhausted."

Christmas was sitting in a chair at the table reading a newspaper out loud, her forefinger tracing each word. She looked up. "What the hell was you doing in there? Sound to me like you all was putting on some kind of floor show or something."

"Wasn't anybody but that Paul, whoever he is."

"Girl, don't pay him no mind. He come in here sometime and he always raising some kind of sand but he always drunk."

"Yes, I know," Eunice said and wandered off to clean the cupboards of the roaches and silverfish that were constantly becoming trapped in the stacked coffee cups.

It was infrequent now that she saw either Pullum or Mrs. Mozique, except on her paydays, and occasionally not even then. Mostly she had to seek them out to get her money, and often she could not find them at all. It did not really matter to her very much, only as a matter of principle, because since she consistently refused to move upstairs, the actual amount of money she received got smaller and smaller. She laughed when she watched Pullum figure out her first pay money. He lowered his trembling bulk into a chair, pulled a pencil from his stained shirt pocket, and began figuring on a napkin that was lying on the tabletop.

"Let see," he mumbled as he licked the tip of the pencil.

"You 'posed to get twenty dollar a week but you eats supper here every day. OK, that a dollar a day for your first eight days."

He wrote carefully:	8.00	eating
	5.50	social securety
	.50	holding taxes
	14.00	

"Fourteen take away twenty, that be six dollar." He reached in a small box of money and gave Eunice six rumpled dollar bills. "There, that be your pay."

Eunice was flabbergasted, but said nothing and pocketed the money.

Pullum looked at her with his round hounddog eyes. "Still don't want to move upstair? You gets more money, plus tips from the customers, and you can be my woman."

"No," Eunice said and walked away.

eleven

*Tell me, baby, what you trying to do, trying to mistreat me,
and I ain't done nothing to you. Mama told me now, I understand. Said if I listen would I play my hand. I know, got to go,
got to go, pretty baby, God knows I ain't lying.*

It was no game, though it often seemed so as they would lie
around the house in their spare time and she stared at him.
"Baby, why you always looking at me?" he would ask.

"I can't see anything better to look at," she would answer.
Each time she looked at him, he was new. A foreign experience.

Looka yonder, what do I see? A whole lots of them running after me.

It became too hard to contain alone and so, in their coupling, Eunice conceived a child.

I'm gone, sure gone, I ain't joking, I ain't jiving, and God knows, I ain't carrying on.

Blacksnake laughed and told her not to worry because when it was born it would be born singing the blues.

I see a whole lot of them coming after me, but I'm gone, yes, baby, and I ain't carrying on.

They were lying on the bed as usual, smoking cigarettes and fingering their quarts of beer. The year, though aging, still was muggy enough so that it was necessary to wear only the barest minimum of clothing. Eunice had brought in some flowers from a nearby vacant lot and after a few hours in the house they were sodden and bent, but with no translatable equation to the bent. Eunice felt vaguely like the flowers.

Somewhere in the recesses of her mind she knew her fibers of toleration were being gnawed thin. She did not question what was happening; she knew she was falling into some deep abyss but dared not incite her mind again to the sense of innocent mystery in this new life she was living for fear she would completely succumb to the hard dictates of it. Not that she would ever forget, but that the sense of her love was being twisted down and forgotten in the drudgery of the days. She knew if she kept on she would soon become merely another acid-lipped woman of Raleigh, filling the days with aimless actions and hurling her body blindly through the nights. She knew it must be ended.

When she had first come here (it had not been long ago) she lay listening to Blacksnake and fascinated by his every movement and turn of mind. Now she began to be scratched by a death she could not pinpoint and did not really want to. It would have been much easier, she thought, not to have attempted in the first place to project energy into either the verb *to jump* or *to fly*, making them transitive and to be acted upon from the moment she stole the record, but she had and it was too late to stop. He criticized her reading (it would give her brain fever) so she had stopped and now lay, not so much looking at him but trying abstractedly to down as much beer as she could, then some whiskey, so she would fall into a deep sleep to take the day swiftly away.

When she worked, which now was sporadic, she worked amidst the gentle haze of many beers and whatever was handy to be got from the men. She had found out it paid to jive with them. Blacksnake talked less these days and often called X. L. to go shoot dice. They lay there drinking themselves into a lethargic frenzy and she knew from the beginning it was not hers to understand but take as it was. Still, it was all perplexing.

Every day now Eunice expanded to the freedom of being outside, even for a moment, and she looked, as did Blacksnake, for any excuse to leave for a while. Every day when she was away she cursed herself for going back to a man with a diamond in his teeth. She cursed herself for not being able to wander off free and thereby nullify his existence.

The children had stopped rolling tires and spinning tops and returned to school. On the first days they looked as if they were going to church: the girls, hair plaited tightly to their heads like farmland seen from an airplane; the boys, duck-bill haircuts greased perpendicular to their scalps and the rest of the head shaved almost clean. Eunice would wander outside in the afternoons, sit on the porch of the house with her guitar, and watch them coming home from school.

One boy she watched particularly. He was about six, with bright-gray eyes and light-brown skin. He always ran past her with a short glance of friendly fear. One day as he passed she laughed and sang to him *Good morning, little schoolboy, good morning, little schoolboy, can I go home with you?*

He stopped and darted around the side of the porch, peeking out.

You tell your mama and your papa, Eunice is a schoolgirl, too.

He edged around the wooden porch post and smiled with his eyes, but his mouth was round with apprehension. Eunice put down the guitar. "Hey, come here."

He edged a bit closer.

"What's your name?"

He said nothing.

"You know, there's a little boy who lives in here, he's smaller than you and he won't talk, either. What's your name?"

He put his hand to his mouth and mumbled.

"What did you say?"

He took his hand away and smiled. "Anth'ny."

"What grade are you in?"

"First."

Eunice laughed and called him to her. He came and she finished the song, then gave him a nickel for candy. After that every afternoon Anthony would be waiting for her at the corner of the porch. Soon other children walking by watched and stopped to listen. As Eunice sang to them they darted into the alley at the side of the porch and tried to dance. She would call them out to dance for her, but they would turn and run off, kicking the dust behind them.

She thought that afternoon that soon she would get up from the bed and go downstairs to wait for Anthony but she lay there and drank more beer. Blacksnake raised an arm in the air and poised his black hand over her stomach. Her quart of beer was almost gone and the chiggers in the flesh at the sides of her stomach were on fire. She felt bloated from the beer and the room was stifling. Dizzily she watched his hand. "You are your own midwife," she said overprecisely, her tongue thick from drinking so much.

His hand trembled a bit. He circled it down slowly to her

stomach and with his fingernail traced around her navel. "Hunh?"

Eunice looked at him and felt old, almost senile. "Nothing. I was just thinking out loud."

"You been reading again." He drew a circle around her navel and hummed *Woman you going to go crazy one of these old days; yes, you going to go crazy, 'cause you got such strange ways.*

"Me?" She put the empty bottle down and her hand groped at the side of the bed for another.

"What you think 'bout this here baby you going to have?"

This was why she could not be free. The denominator was zero. She took his finger in her hand and traced with him widening circles on her belly. He hummed on, saying various things, and she thought of those treasonous blues and the man weaving sabotage in her with the craft of his hands. But she loved him and his strange statements of essence, his blues, and her tired fingers helped his walk like unsuspecting feet over a minefield. "I don't know about it."

He stopped and rested his hand on her stomach. "Well, I does. It ain't going to have no worry. It going to be just exactly like me."

She laughed with him, but out of fear, because she knew she would be the one who would have to teach it the ways of this man and make it know no other. "Yes, I suppose so."

" 'Course it is, baby. Naw, it ain't going to have *no* worry." There was a knock on the door. "That 'bout to be old X. L. Baby, go get the door for your sweet daddy."

"All right."

She put the beer down and started to heave herself off the bed, but he grasped her and held her to him so she could not breathe. He said nothing but he was shaking and she knew he was trying with all the strength in him to know, to be sure of the fact that she was his, and that he could not understand the change. He let her go suddenly and lay back on the bed. For the first time, and for the last, she saw sadness in his eyes. Perpetually he was screaming of a derelict heart, but it was always with a pride and exultation that conquered the sadness by its very shout: *Baby, please don't go, you know it hurts me so.* Now there was no need for words. He knew; she realized that she would go, and he would drive her to go, but she would not go home, she would merely go on.

"All right, baby, all right," he whispered, looking at her with his great sad eyes. He slammed the beer bottle down on the floor.

The doorbell rang again. Eunice cracked the door. "Yes?"

"Ma'm, I'm here representing the coordinated civil rights groups of this city. We're making an organized drive to have everyone registered before the coming election. We realize, and we would like to impress upon you, the fact that it is important for you to register so that your conditions of living will be raised and you will gain political and economic freedom, so that you may become first-class citizens."

"Oh," Eunice said and looked at the stringy-haired, salmon-hued young man standing in the doorway with a large pad of paper resting in the crook of his knobby arm.

"Hm, yes. Well, we'd like to register you—that is, if you aren't registered already."

"No, I'm not."

"Well, I'm sure you know how important it is for all Negroes to be registered. Look outside. Here in this part of town you have no sidewalks and on the main street they are badly in need of repair. You have no adequate lighting and the neighborhood children are forced to play in the gutters. If you register you can work together to get better facilities for the entire neighborhood."

Eunice surveyed the man and thought of the red roads that were streets. "I don't want to register."

The boy shifted from one flat foot to another and scratched

a festering pimple. "But ma'm, it's important that you try and better your society. Can't you see that?"

"No, I can't."

He paused a moment, and then proceeded. "Whatever your hesitation stems from, it is not good. It is necessary for us all to work together in obtaining the common goal of equality. It is not only equality in spirit; your living standards must be equal. Environment plays an important factor. You must realize also that it is not only your right but your duty to choose the people you wish to represent you in our government. If you do not vote you have no choice in determining how you will live."

Eunice chuckled as she remembered Bertha back in the jail. She crinkled her eyes and laughed. "Well, sho is, ain't it."

The young man stepped back a bit from the door and looked at her. "Ma'm, we're *trying* to help you."

"Yeah, sho is, ain't you." Eunice laughed and felt the beer spring to her head. She reeled slightly as he peered in the door.

"Um, your husband. Is he registered?"

Eunice abruptly stopped laughing. She called to Blacksnake. "Do you want to register to vote?"

"Naw, baby," he yelled. "I got no time."

"Well, ma'm," the young man persisted. "It *is* important."

Eunice was tired of hanging on the doorknob for support. She wanted to lie down. "No, thank you, not today. Come back when you're selling tomatoes." She slammed the door in his face.

Blacksnake raised up. "What he want?"

"He wanted us to register to vote."

"Oh, shit. Woman, I can't vote. I been to the penitench."

"That's right. When you've gone there you can't vote."

"I 'poses it a good thing. I done change my name and vote for Roosevelt but he dead now and I doesn't bother 'bout nobody else. 'Sides, I doesn't want them white folks come messing 'round here too much. I likes to keep my business to myself. Is you going to vote?"

"No."

"Why?"

"I've got my reasons."

"Oh, that right. You ain't ole enough nohow."

"No, but that's not the reason. It's just that everything's ridiculous, from getting up in the morning to washing my face and going to bed at night, and everybody does that everywhere no matter where they are."

"Shit, not me, baby. My automobile get more washing than I ever does."

"That's not what I'm talking about. I mean everybody's going to end up doing the same old things everybody else does whether they're rich or poor so it doesn't make any difference. You've got to shit just the same as the President does."

"I still doesn't understand, but if you gots your reasons, you gots your reasons. It just seem like you don't tell your old daddy nothing no more."

"That's what I mean, anyhow."

"Girl, you got some strange things turning 'round in that head of yours. Why *did* you come here anyway?"

"I don't know. I just felt like it."

Eunice sat down on the bed and scratched her head. It was useless to try and find the causes of her being here; she merely was and could never be sure whether it was a true act or a posture of defiance.

Though what she had left had been a perceivable thing, she could not tell if that was a true act either or a mass gesture to a defiance of some other thing. So her commitment against it had to begin and grow from the same consciousness that society had acted upon.

Since her parents had built and waged life within their framework, in order to obvert it fully she, too, had to build or find a counterstructure and exist within it at all costs. The difference lay in that theirs was predicated on a pseudo-rationality whereas the rational was neither integral nor peripheral in hers; she did not consider it at all. To her the excesses of the heart had to be able to run rampant and find their own boundaries, exhausting themselves in plaguing hope.

Blacksnake looked at her. "What you thinking 'bout now, girl?"

"Oh, nothing much."

"Well, stop thinking and tell me what it like out there in Frisco."

"I don't like it, it's too cold and crowded."

"I think I be 'bout to like it. Maybe you can carry me there someday. I'd like to be seeing them states. I been 'bout all over the South, but I ain't been neither nor East or West. Is you ever been to New Yorks?"

"No, and I don't particularly want to."

"Well, I hears that a fine place. They got buildings so high you can't see where they ends. Maybe they just goes on up into the sky. And they tells me there so much money it just fall on down like that manna did for them Jews a long time ago."

"I guess so, but I still don't want to go there. I like it here."

"Girl, you crazy to like it down here. The South ain't no good. You knows where Jacqueline come from, over to Monroe, they got lots of them night riders. It ain't no black man safe there. You could get youself kill and wouldn't nobody even know of your death. Man, when that old X. L. coming?"

"I don't know."

"Shit, you ain't 'posed to know. Look like I'm got to join them night riders myself to get a little action out of these slow-assed niggers what call themself my friends. That 'cludes you, too."

"Me?"

"Yeah, you, baby. I don't be knowing what wrong with you

but you acting so funny till I just don't know what to do."

"Well, you're always going off with X. L. to gamble and I don't know what."

Fiercely he took her face in his hands and smiled painfully. "Baby, I don't know nothing else to do. I been doing it all my black life."

twelve

Often they would go and see Blacksnake's mother. Every
time they came she would lay her hands on Eunice's stomach
and bless the unformed child. She would talk to it as if it were
holding on to Eunice's hand, waiting bashfully for a piece of
candy, then she would scold it much as she must have scolded
Blacksnake. She was an old woman, forgetful and black. She
patted Eunice's head, called her "girl," and told her to always
come to see her because Snake, her boy, was bad. Eunice
would sometimes go alone to Mama's house to wash her
clothes and comb her hair. Mama enjoyed it, blessed her belly
again, and smiled.

Autumn in Raleigh was a strange time. Blacksnake's mood cooled as did the season. The leaves on the trees reddened, withered, and dropped to the ground. Blacksnake slackened his playing and began coming in the Raleigh Palace Bar to watch Eunice work. He would wander in with X. L. to shoot pool and drink. He would look at Eunice out of the corner of his eye, leave just before she got off work, and meet her back at the house.

At first when she would return he would look at her and ask, "Woman, you have yourself a good time today?"

She told him repeatedly the work was hard and she felt uncomfortable at having to put up with the words and actions of the men customers.

"Yeah, the mens is what I's *talking* 'bout," he would say with an edge to his voice. "You have a good time jiving with the mens?"

Eunice was beginning to become conscious of the growing weight inside her and would sit on the bed beside him. "No, I told you, I'm tired of fooling with those men who come in there."

"What you means you tired of mens? Don't look like you fixing to lay off them for a while. Ain't that why you got the job? Don't look like you so tired of them mens as you is tired of poor me. They must work you pretty hard, you so damn dead when you comes back here."

Eunice was even too tired to answer. She sighed.

He eyed her. "Woman, doesn't you hear me axing you a question?"

"Yes, of course I hear you," she snapped. "You've taken to coming in there so much it seems to me you ought to know what I do. You see me carrying beer back and forth and wiping off tables."

"All I sees is you sidling up to them mens."

"Mrs. Mozique makes me. I don't like to but she makes me."

"Shit, she make you like I make you. You's just nothing but a fool."

"What's the matter with you? You're getting strange-acting. Do you want me to go?"

He straightened up. "*No,* I just wants you to straighten up and fly right and quit slipping 'round behind my back all times of the day and night, evil-hearted woman that you is."

Eunice would not answer but would get up and cook him something. He would noisily gulp his food down and wander out, often not returning until late.

When he returned, Eunice usually would be asleep. He would roughly wake her up. "Goddamn, woman, why you sleeping? Doesn't you know you's 'posed to be up ready to open the door for me when I comes in, and have me a hot cup of something?"

Eunice would sit up and wipe sleep from her eyes. "Well, I was tired. I've got to work in the morning."

He bent over her, smelling of whiskey and wine. "Naw, I says you to *wait* up for me."

"All right," Eunice would say and fall back to sleep.

The next time she would remain awake, rummaging through his drawers in hope of finding something to read. He would come in and say, "Goddamn, woman, why ain't you in bed sleeping like you 'posed to do?"

Exasperated, Eunice would face him. "Last time you told me to wait up for you."

"Shit, I bets your back-door man just left. I done *told* you I don't want nobody in this house 'cept who I says, and here you goes slipping some man in whilst I's gone down the road." He would check everything in the closet, look under the bed and in the kitchen, cursing to himself.

Eunice would watch him and when he was through she would say, "You don't like it when I stay awake and you don't like it when I go to sleep. What do you want me to do?"

"Shit, I just knows you done had a man up here; you ain't

fooling old me. Remember I's the *Blacksnake*, and don't nothing slip away from this nigger."

"I don't want any other man. Besides, I wouldn't be that stupid if I did, to bring one up here."

He would look tiredly at her and scratch his head. "Well, perhaps you's right. You better go on to sleep. That way I knows you ain't been doing nothing behind my back."

Eunice would take off her clothes and lie down, too tired to argue. "All right. Have it as you wish, I don't care."

One evening he came in very late, clattering up the stairs and banging on the door. Eunice awoke to the noise. He stood in the doorway, tall and black, with his green mohair homburg askew. He lurched in the door, grabbed her arm, and held it fiercely. "Woman, I *knows,* I just *knows* you done just had some man up here."

Eunice sat up. "What do you mean?"

His forehead faulted. "Goddamn, I knows them peoples you works with. You ain't doing nothing but ruining yourself 'sociating with them, and now one of them been up here with you. I can tell it."

Eunice tried to twist out of his grasp, but he only pinioned her tighter. "Let go," she moaned. "You know I don't have any other man."

He grabbed her other arm. "You *lie,* woman." She struggled to protest but before she could say anything he slapped her across the mouth. "Just don't say one Goddamn thing, not a thing. I knows all about you and your high-yellow ways."

He released her and reached for his guitar. *I gots womens upstairs, I gots womens downstairs, I gots womens across the street. Yes, Lord, I gots womens upstairs, womens downstairs, and womens across the street. And, Eunice, if you don't quit mistreating me I'm got to go get me some other good pig meat.*

Eunice reached for her clothes. She held her mouth. Her lips stung and she was more surprised than angry. "What the hell are you doing?"

Tell me, woman, what did you do tonight? Please, tell me what did you do tonight? You know your hair all tangled and you just ain't talking right.

He turned around. "Where you intending to go, back to the Raleigh Funk House or back to your lying mama? *Oh, yes, I believes you better go home to your mama, 'cause I can't use you. Yes, you better go on home to your mama, little girl, 'cause I can't use you no more. Then I can go out and love all them pretty womens what is lined up outside my back door."*

Eunice whirled around and walked toward him. "What the shit *is* wrong with you?"

He grabbed her already sore wrist and twisted her down by him. His mouth curled and the diamond was half exposed. "It ain't what wrong with me, baby," he said slowly and precisely, "it what wrong with you. What make you come here in the first place with your lying ass? I been thinking 'bout it for a long long old time. I done talked it over with X. L. and we can't figure you out. *I knows you used to love me, baby, but I believe you don't love me now, yes, I thinks you don't love me now. You acting so funny, you don't need a good man nohow."*

Eunice looked at him and wept because she could not explain. She knew there was sense somewhere but it was not speakable. It was lost down in the marrow of the blues Blacksnake and X. L. sang and it was the vague but pungent taste of that which had sent her down here precisely to love this man.

He turned to her. "You does love me, but you's so evil that I guesses I'm got to whip you every morning and beat you late every night. I got to do you just like a baby child to make you treat me right." He got his handkerchief out of his pocket and wiped her eyes. "I thought I done told you not to cry. Don't get off your base now, woman."

Then he became embarrassed because he saw she would not stop, and held her close, singing *When I come home this evening, I found my little baby crying; when I come to my home this evening, I found my little baby crying. I axed her what was the matter and she say I just wonder what have happen to that loving man of mine.*

He lay back on the bed and drew her to him, her body scraping against the rough texture of his clothes. "Hush, woman, and go to sleep."

The next morning Eunice sat on the porch. She waited all day with a large whiskey bottle at her side and by the time she saw the schoolchildren coming home it was almost gone. She could hardly see, her head was pounding so hard.

Anthony skipped up to her. "Ain't you going to sing for me today, ma'm?"

She slipped on a pair of sunglasses and looked at him. "Come here, Anthony, and sit down." He sat on the steps beside her. "Listen, can you and some of your friends do a favor for me?"

He looked at her. "Yessir, ma'm."

"Well, I want you to do it right now, and then come back here. I'll be waiting for you."

"What you want?"

"You go get a paper sack and take some friends and catch me a rattlesnake. Don't you kill it, just catch it and bring it back to me alive, hear? I'll give you each fifty cents."

"Yessir, ma'm, but what you want a rattler for? Them's poison."

"Never mind, just go do what I tell you and come back as soon as you can. I'll be waiting right here."

Anthony ran off and came back in a while with two other boys. He was holding the bag on the end of a long stick. Eunice took the sack and opened it slightly, then she gave them their money. They ran off to the store. She looked in the bag again. A gray-brown snake was curled inside. She went upstairs and got a piece of paper and a pen. Her lips were wet and she was biting them unconsciously as she carefully wrote three times:

blacksnake brown
ekanskcalb nworb
Ito, alto Massa Dandi
Bando, III, Lit. Dominus vobiscum, unay. Amen

She was so drunk she was laughing at herself, and to continue she had to take another drink and force herself into a frenzy of quiet madness. She got a small black bag out from under her side of the bed, and some string from the kitchen. Then she turned off the lights and walked down the steps to the street.

She paraded down the street, drunk and feeling very much like a demon queen sent to placate her god for the permission to be for a time with this man. It was dusk and she felt the warmth of the city as people were returning from work. As she walked down the road, lights in shabby houses came on and a warm odor of all kinds of cooking attacked her nostrils. Occasionally the snake rustled in the bag.

Eunice slipped around a corner and took another drink of whiskey. She had had so much she felt like going off in the bushes and sleeping, but the new burning took away even that and dulled her to every want except the one at hand.

She went to a vacant lot in Evan's Bottom. It was a tangle of trees and vines and a narrow path led through the jungle of green. A small sewage creek crisscrossed the path, disappearing after every crossing into the brush. Eunice pushed her way through the vines and ivy that dropped from the trees until she came to a junction with another path. Outside of this small clearing was nothing but foliage reaching high above her.

A large tree marked this junction, its roots knotting down to the smelly bilge-water stream. She walked to the edge and got a rock. She took it and pounded on the bag until the movement inside stopped. Then she opened the bag and held the dead snake by its head.

She cut off the rattles and put them in her pocket. With her fingers she pried the mouth open, stuffed the paper and black bag in, and wrapped it shut with the string. Then she made a hole in the skin just below the bloody stump where the rattles had been, drew the string through it, and secured it to a limb of the tree. She threw the rock in the brackish water, sat down at the foot of the tree and began to cry.

Eunice woke up and looked around. It was dark. She didn't know how long she had been there. Her body ached where she had lain against the tree's exposed roots. She looked up and saw the dangling snake. Bracing herself against the trunk, she pulled up. Involuntarily her hands moved to untie the snake; then she remembered that she had put it there, and smiling tiredly, she walked away.

When she got back to the room she saw that Blacksnake was asleep. Silently she dumped the rattles into the body of her guitar, took off her clothes, and heaved herself into bed next to him. It creaked and he shot up.

"Goddamn it, woman, where you been with your yellow ass?"

Eunice tiredly turned over. "Mmmm?"

He snapped the back of his hand hard at her head. "I said *where* you been until this time of night? I ain't had nothing to eat. A woman 'posed to tend to her man, but you's just like all the rest of them yellow gals; get you a man and you can't do nothing but run out to mistreat him. Shit."

Eunice looked at him and knew she still loved him. "I've been out walking. I got tired of waiting for you."

He slapped her and pushed her away from him. "Shit, I ain't taking no more of your raising sand in a high-assed fashion. I comes home and wants my *food,* and what you out doing? You out walking the streets. If that ain't the pig's titty. Fix me something to eat, *now!"* Eunice rolled out of the bed and grabbed a robe. She went to the kitchen and got a can of beef soup and put it on the stove. Blacksnake followed her and stuck his head over her shoulder, breathing heavily. 'Now, what the hell you think you doing? Can't even fix a fucking can of soup. I bets you trying to slip something into it. I's going to watch you every minute of your poor-assed life."

Eunice turned around. "I'm doing the *best* I can."

"Well, that just ain't *good* enough. Lookit, you's scalding the soup. I ain't going to eat none. It ain't fit to eat. If you wasn't out co'ting somebody else you wouldn't be so motherfucking tired. I doesn't know why you's here anyhow."

Eunice got a bowl, poured some soup into it, and handed it to the Blacksnake. "If that isn't enough I'll fix you something else."

He banged the bowl down on the table. "Something else? Something *else.* The way you screwed this shit up I wouldn't trust you boiling Goddamn water. Where your bowl? I ain't going to touch this here till you eats some first. Then if you don't fall dead, maybe I try some."

He walked back to the bedroom calling over his shoulder *Baby, I just want to know why. When you gots all them wells to draw water from, you insist upon drawing water from my poor eyes.*

She called after him, "I'm not going to poison you."

He sat down on the bed, then reared up and shook a long finger at her. *Yes, tell me why, woman, you insist upon drawing water from Blacksnake's eyes.*

Hiking up his too big pajama bottoms, he shook the bowl of soup at her, stamping the floor with his knotted feet. "Shut up. Just shut up. Get you a bowl of this shit and come on back to the bed. I's so sick of your ways I might die 'fore my time out of worrying what you up to next."

They ate in silence. Then Eunice turned off the light and lay back down in bed. "Good night."

"Good night? Woman, you thinks I'm going to sleep with a damn desperator next to me? Goddamn, no telling what you might do for all your nappy-headed lover mens out on the streets. Might come in and rob me. Shit."

Eunice twitched angrily. "People don't accuse like that unless they've got their own dirty business."

He sent a stinging slap to her face. "*You* 'cusing *me?* Why, I's so good to your poor self I could cry every time I thinks 'bout it, so don't you talk none 'bout my business. What I been doing I been doing it all my life and I ain't going to stop. Every woman I ever had I treats her right, and I had aplenty, believe me, baby! In all my time here I ain't met one yet who would try and do me good like I done her, but you's the worst of them all. Come here from the West Coasts, might be like Russia or something, it so fucking far off. I doesn't know nothing 'bout you and you come here and run after me like you ain't never seen a man before. I believes you a spy or something." He stopped and scratched his chin. "Yeah, you must be one of them spies. Goddamn, if that ain't something."

He lunged to hit her again, but she jumped out of the bed. "All right, I'll leave. I'm sick and tired of your jaw-jooking and crazy talking all the time. If I tried to explain you wouldn't understand. You have the hardest black head I've ever seen."

"Goddamn it, *go* then! You *never* find a home as good as this. *I'm got to say, bye-bye, baby, be on your way. Just don't come crying to the Blacksnake some old rainy day.*"

Eunice sat on the edge of the bed and put her clothes on. She could barely see them she was crying so hard. "I'm going, I'm going. Just shut up and let me leave in peace."

As she moved toward her things, he watched her. "In peace? Shit, you wants to go in peace after you done run me insane with your shit? Ha, is you a motherfucker."

Eunice slammed the door behind him and sat down on the landing. The night was not cold but she was shivering. She cried softly to herself until she was cried out and there was only a desperate moan before she dozed.

Behind her she heard the door open and Blacksnake pad up. He bent over her, and extending his hands under her arms, lifted her up. "Come on in this house, woman. What the peoples going to say, you sitting out on my porch like a lonesome child? Get in the bed and quit acting like a fool."

As he set her on the bed and undressed her, Eunice tried to see his face, but whenever she looked up he seemed to be grimacing and the radiance of the diamond made her only able to see his face as patches of black. "All right now, come on over here next to me."

Eunice started crying again softly as he held her and kissed her forehead, stroking the damp hair from her face. "Now, baby, why you want to do me that way?"

"I don't know," she mumbled into his chest as she struggled to lose herself completely in him, to become so completely joined to him there was no differentiation of body or mind. She gritted her teeth, ground them, cursed, and called to God at the same time, but still she was completely herself. When he had finally fallen asleep, she disengaged herself from him and slipped out of the bed. Quietly she put her clothes on and went out in the early morning.

It is too complex, too deceivable, she thought, too real. You pulse with too much life, too much hate for death. Nothing grips your soul but life, innocent and demanding as a child. It is I who am old, who have the smell of death. You taught me to jive to life, but you taught it to me too late; I cannot stay both captive and alive.

So sorry, man, but thank you. Thank you for blasting me down to grope where there was a beating, but not yet blues. You rode me, easy-riding daddy, and let me taste your empti-ness, let me taste it slowly and make new blues from the sweet, sweet flavor of you, easy-riding man.

Good-bye.

part **two** *so sorry to leave you, baby*

thirteen

Again it was the same terrain to be covered by train. The placating autumn rain had jested with the country and the people; one would believe the life was as gentle as the deceivingly soft countryside and even the terror of the thick gray swamps appeared to be of an inviting sort. But it was as much a lie as the faces of the people, looking as if they were capable of experiencing only bland emotions when in reality violence was vulgarly raked from every scrap of life and exploded as suddenly and as effectively as the thunderstorms redundantly assailing the countryside. Eunice looked out of the window. Everything above the wall of trees was insipid blue, but just ahead were banks of huge clouds, coal-colored at the top, turning into violet and red as they cascaded over one another.

She thought of her first trip from Lake Charles and the sober determination to possess the man she had not seen. She had not believed then that she was actually leaving, for she had dreamed it so much. Dreamed of walking down the empty street, her heels clouting the bare sidewalk in the chill dawn air, and singing her leaving blues to a rising sun. She knew it had been a fakery of sorts, watching herself move slowly down the dawn-lit street with the sun a burning cavern, feeble still in the cool sky and shining somberly down on the houses, giving the whole neighborhood the appearance of a deserted monastery.

And it had been a fakery, a handy purchase of one absolute gratuity for another. Even the vultures waited for their prey to die, but being young, she was impatient like a jackal and she couldn't have waited any longer for maturity to make her more prudent or more lazy. She had to leave quickly or not at all.

Now, again, she had to leave quickly and she departed Raleigh like some senile Columbus, across the land, putting great distance between her and Blacksnake. There was no sense, she knew, in going back to San Francisco, back home to bring a child into a world of people who were too much and only in awe of their own consciousness. They were as rigid and sterile as the buildings that towered above them.

The train headed on toward Lake Charles. She remembered, from the last time, the rough-hewn street with all its indefinite, wildly growing shrubbery that had a precisely defined quality as if it were lodged in the middle of an ice cube or enclosed within a piece of cellophane. It was a street to look at but not to live on, or even to walk down. Nevertheless, she had turned onto this street, killing time between trains.

It had been noon and everything was quiet under the cracking light. Huge shingled houses were set back from the pathways. Evidently these once had been the fine homes of whites; now room-for-rent signs hung from the doors like smears of jam on children's faces. Trash and garbage littered the street and the sidewalk was broken and damaged. On one house, a large green house with chipping red trim, hung a sign:

Madame Karplus
Spiritual Mother from
INDIA
No Appt. Nec.

Eunice had glanced at her watch; she still had forty-five minutes before the L&N rolled in for Mississippi, Carolina, and points east. She opened the rusting wrought-iron gate, trampling weeds, and pulled on the huge corroding knocker on the door. She heard creaking inside and the door opened. A large yellow woman stood in the doorway. "What can I do for you?"

She had tried to peer beyond the woman into the house but the woman's form seemed to flow with her eyes, blocking any view beyond a faded blue mammy dress, sagging and ripped at the waist. "Well, it says that you're a spiritual adviser on the sign outside."

"Yes."

Again she had bent a bit, trying to see through the small space between the woman's crossed arm. She tried to think of something to say. Only an impetuous sense to grab a taste of the mysterious had egged her to the door. "I'm waiting between trains, and I wondered if you could tell my fortune."

The woman drew back her full lips and spat far out onto the burnt lawn. "Come on in."

Eunice followed her through a high, spacious room, filled with red and black burning candles. The room drew its only light from these, for the windowpanes were painted black. A sweetly strong heavy odor of incense and perfume hung at about nose level. She coughed and followed the woman into the kitchen.

The floor was highly polished linoleum of indeterminable pattern. The woman indicated that Eunice sit in a straight-backed chair at a small kitchen table covered with a plastic tablecloth. Here, also, the window shades were drawn. Various candles burned in front of statues and the stench of incense was overpowering. Eunice sat in the chair and eased it up to the table with her feet. The woman leaned against the stove and looked down at Eunice. "Now, whatever you wants, it do be five dollar."

"Well, actually, ma'm, I want to find out what you do."

The woman drew back her lips and laughed. "You crazy. I just be telling peoples' fortune to help them out of trouble and strife in this life. That all."

Eunice glanced at the flickering candles. "How do you do it?"

The woman shot her a cold look. "What you think? 'Course with the cards and the hor'scopes."

Eunice looked again at the candles and the statues of strange saints playing in and out of vision as the flames shifted. "Can you get me a bone?"

Madame Karplus laughed again. She jerked her bulk off the stove and replanted it in a chair opposite Eunice. Still laughing, she reached out and took hold of Eunice's fingers, examining them in the lowly jaundiced light. "Hé, you come to the right place then. I'm got one."

She got up, went to a cupboard, and began taking various things down, setting them on the drainboard below. She gathered them in her arms and put them on the table. First, she took three black candles and set them in a small triangle in the center of the table. In the middle she placed one red candle. She had long slender hands that seemed not to belong to her mulelike body, and they moved with a dance of their own arranging crackers, bottles, powders, oils, and other articles around the candles.

Madame Karplus sat down and lit the candles. She placed a statue next to the red candle and began softly to intone: *Eh, yé yé, Mamzelle Marie.* She reached in her pocket and took out a small chamois bag, then she picked up a small dish with oil in it and passed it over the flame three times. "This Luck Master oil," she said and rubbed some into the bag. "Oh, St. Expédite, make us stout of heart."

From another plate she retrieved a small piece of yellow rock. "This Lodestone." She placed it at the bottom of the bag. "Oh, St. Expédite, give us success." She took up another dish, passed it three times over the flame, reached in and pinched some fine grayish powder into the bag. She dipped her fingers into the dish again and blew the residue at Eunice, saying, "Oh, St. Expédite, give us power to speak for what we wants." Then she took an empty bowl from the table and slipped out of the room.

Outside, Eunice heard a short scuffling, and in a moment Madame Karplus returned with the bowl. "This dove blood. Lean over so I can make a cross." Eunice leaned over; the woman dipped her forefinger in the bowl, and traced three crosses on Eunice's forehead. "Now you puts your mark with this here dove blood on a paper, you do it three time forward and three time backward."

She handed Eunice paper and a stick. When Eunice had done as she directed, Madame Karplus sprinkled more Luck Master oil on the paper, rolled it up, reached for a small bone and forced the paper into the empty marrow shaft. She took the red candle, let it drip on the bone to seal the hole, then let a drop of black wax fall on top of the red. "Oh, St. Expédite, let this be a lucky hand."

She reached in her pocket and took out a small nodule, knobby and brown as a withered peach seed. "This a High John the Conquerer root." She placed it in the bag and put the bone on top of it. Her fingers moved again as she sewed the bag up. "Oh, St. Expédite, let us hold everything done in this bag." She passed three times over the flame and set the bag at the foot of the St. Expédite statue. "You is to keep the hand where you can always touch it. 'Bove all, don't let nobody know what you got. 'Member, you gots a Black Cat bone so if you ever wants somebody to have bad luck, just take this here hand and get you a rattlesnake. Kill it and shove the hand down its mouth."

She paused and wrote something on a piece of paper. She handed it to Eunice. "Write this here on a paper and write the name of the person you wants to have the bad luck on the same paper three time backward and three time forward and shove this down the snake's mouth, too. Then cut off the rattles, save them, and hang the carcass on a tree someplace. Call on St. Expédite to help you. And soon as that snake wither up to bone, whoever you want to have the bad luck going to wither up and die, too." She blew out the candles and stood up. "I 'spects you'm got to get that train." She walked to the door and Eunice followed, gripping the small bag in her hand.

Outside, the precision of the surroundings had dissipated. The street had seemed to laugh at her and the weeds had rustled dryly.

This time the train slipped into Lake Charles late in the night. Outside it was cold, but the people seemed active and flaunting their warmth against the chill. Eunice got off the train and did not think of anything except to eat. She was dazed and disembodied from herself and watched her actions, so precise and dry, as if she were only in obeisance to a predetermined pattern. But this time she believed in the actuality of her motions as she checked her bags and went to investigate the town again.

She walked into a small café near the station, ordered hog maws and greens, then went over to the jukebox. She put a quarter in, selected several records, and sat down to eat. The greens were saturated with stale grease and salt pork but she ate them. She glanced up and saw a young soldier at the counter watching her. She did not acknowledge his presence as she went on forcing herself to chew the food. He came over and sat down as she was finishing.

"Have a cigarette?"

"All right."

She took the cigarette and got up to leave. "Here, I'll pay for it."

"All right."

He paid the bill and they walked out. "Where you wants to go for something to drink?"

"I don't really know the town. Anywhere'll be all right."

"Well, I knows a place," the soldier said as he guided her to a dark beer joint.

They went in and had a beer in silence. Lake Charles reminded her of some old desert town on the California-Nevada border. Even though it was near. water and the surrounding area was green, it seemed a dry, stark place. Awnings of wood and canvas extended from the building fronts to the curb, and sidewalks, when there were any, were conspicuously elevated, making one feel as if one were walking in a tube.

A zotico band unpacked and set up to play.

"Where you coming from?" the soldier asked.

"Raleigh."

"Where you going to?"

"I don't know."

"Look to me like you ought to be from someplace 'round here."

"No, my mother came from Lafayette, but not me."

"Well, I 'spected as much."

He ordered two more beers. The band started its scratching, animal beat with the rub board and concertina. The man playing the concertina made unintelligible sounds to the *chooka-chooka* of the rub board.

"Let's dance," the soldier said and propelled Eunice to her

feet. They began shuffling to the beat until it possessed their movements and they fell into a bizarre rocking, held completely in sway by the pounding rub board. The music went on and on, never stopping, the beat pounding louder and louder. People here and there were dropping out, exhausted, to sip a beer and then resume their ritualistic turnings.

Eunice sat down and sighed to catch her breath. "Get me another beer, will you?"

"Yeah, sure," the soldier said. Sweat and grease from his hair was darkening his collar, and his neck was throbbing. They drank the beer and then he got a bottle of whiskey. The music kept pulsing and talk was only possible if one screamed.

"It's getting late, let's go," the soldier said.

"Where?"

"I don't know. I knows a place over to Beaudry where we can go."

"No."

"Why not?"

"Just no."

"I give you ten dollar."

"No, thanks."

They drank some more whiskey and listened to the music.

"You sure you don't wants to go?"

"I'm sure."

"I give you fifteen dollar."

"No, thanks."

"I just got pay, you know, and I's out on leave for a few days."

"That's nice, but still no."

"Won't you at least come with me to Beaudry and stay? I give you fifteen dollars for that, 'cause I been looking for someone nice like you."

"Thank you, no." The soldier was beginning to grate on Eunice. She drank more whiskey.

"I give you twenty-five dollar if you just come and talk to me. We can sit in a room and talk till the morning come."

"Why do you want to talk?"

"I been lonesome since I came to this town. I ain't had nobody to keep me company."

"I don't feel like talking."

"Don't you need no money? I give you thirty dollar, now, if you just come sit with me and talk."

"*No*, thank you."

"If you comes with me, I do anything you want to make you happy. Whatever you wants done, I make you happy for tonight."

Eunice smiled disgustedly. "I said I don't care to go with you."

"I don't know nobody here. I's from Opelousas."

"Perhaps, then, you better go back there. It's not far."

"Yeah, I knows, but it ain't nothing there. That ain't nothing but a country crossroads." He took her hand. "Won't you come with me, please?"

"All right, I'll go with you, but just to talk."

"Good, let's go."

"I don't want to go as far as Beaudry, though."

He paused a moment. "Oh, say, they gots rooms upstair where we can go, I done forgot about that." He paid the bill and Eunice followed him upstairs. He knocked on the first door. A short round woman peeked out.

"Oh, hi, you wants a room? Three dollar a night." She handed him a key. "Number fifty-five." The soldier gave her the money and she closed a freckled brown fist over it and locked the door.

They walked down the narrow long hallway. There were no carpets and their feet on the buckling boards made the floor sound as if it were constipated. The house reeked of stale bodies and reminded her of a summer long ago near the Gulf where her parents had brought her when she was seven or eight.

She had played with the neighborhood children in the streets and alleys and once they had wandered off to play. They threw stones and ran to places they had never been before on the other side of the town. Then one of them noticed a two-story gray house that appeared abandoned. They decided to investigate and Eunice, eager to be accepted as one of them, took the first dare. She remembered how the house had stood alone at the end of the block—tall, gray, and reeking a sense of forbidding.

She had been shaking as she approached but she could hear the others goading her on. She went to the cloth that served as a door and pushed it aside. There was a long hallway leading to a stairs. She crept up them, ready for the slightest sound to send her running out. Everything was quiet and the house stank subtly, as did this hotel. When she reached the top of the stairs a small gate blocked further movements.

She had turned to run out but as her eyes became accustomed to the sickly light she noticed a shadow move behind a half-opened door in front of her. Then she looked around and saw that six or seven doors lined the upper floor, some closed and others cracked open. She saw no one but as she stood there she could barely hear soft voices behind the doors, though they seemed only sounds suspended in the hall. She backed down the steps, certain now that someone lived there, and fascinated because no one had come out to chase her away. And as she tiptoed out she saw a figure come out of one of the rooms and she broke into a run.

She had returned to her friends and everyone had wanted to go in then. But as they approached the house a steel-haired man in a greasy T-shirt walked out. They hid at the corner of the house, crouching on the ground. Just then above them they heard laughter, and as they backed away they saw through the low window above them four fat women lying on beds.

They were in various states of undress, shaking and slapping each other and laughing hysterically. One of them leaned out of the window and called to a boy in the group. "Hey, honey, come here!" He took a step forward, but the others held him back. "Hey, boy, don't you be a-scared of me. I ain't going to hurt you none."

She turned back to the other women. "Looka here, ain't he fine, young, and sweet? Nothing too young for me. I give him my piece for free. Shit, I even pay *him!*" They laughed and slapped one another again and Eunice and the children had run away as fast as they could.

The soldier unlocked the cracked painted door and they went in. The wallpaper was damp and discolored, long brownish stains marking the juncture of the strips. There was a small warped table next to the bed, where the only light, a rusted snake-neck lamp, drooped from its resting place. Strangely enough, brightly colored plastic curtains hung from the one filthy window. Eunice wondered if the rooms in the house so long ago had been like this.

There was an overpowering smell of gas in the room. The soldier bent over a dented gas stove and lit a match and a blue flame darted out.

Eunice took her jacket off and sat down on a straight-backed chair by the bed. The ribs of the chair dug into her buttocks and spine, but she remained with her hands folded tightly in her lap. The soldier tossed his hat on the floor and stretched out on the bed. "Why you don't come over here and sit down?"

Eunice tilted her head back and looked at the sagging stained ceiling. "I'm comfortable here." She yawned and a cramp constricted her throat.

"Yeah," said the soldier, "but I wants to talk to you."

The cramp subsided slowly and Eunice saw that he was very young, about eighteen, her age. "I can hear you well enough from here, thank you."

She was tense, not with fear but with boredom and the

tired foreknowledge of his plan. She laughed softly to herself. "Do you want me to go to bed with you?"

He propped his head up. "Hunh?"

The corners of her mouth pinched up to stop the rising laughter. "I asked you did you want me to go to bed with you?" And without waiting for an answer she walked over to the bed.

He watched her with surprise. "Why you have to say it that way? I thought we was going to talk some and then maybe we could work around a bit."

Eunice stood over the bed and snorted. "Well, make up your mind. I don't want to waste time either way."

"Sweetcakes, is you trying to play some kind of game or something?"

Eunice laughed. "No. By all your hemming and hawing you just lost your chance for salvation." She sat down on the bed. "OK. Thirty dollars for some talk. What do you want to talk about?"

He scratched his head in bewilderment. "I doesn't understand what you doing, but that all right. What *you* want to talk 'bout?"

Eunice began picking at the knots on the bedspread. "It's your money, you decide. I could just as soon go to sleep."

His hand grasped her forearm. "You knows, I sure is glad you come up here and stay with me. Otherwise I wouldn't have nobody to talk to. Wherever you going, can I go, too? You nice."

"I don't know where I'm going, and I don't think I'd want you to come with me. I can't be bothered."

"You say your mama come from Lafayette?"

"Yes?"

"What your last name?"

"Prideaux."

"Mmm. I don't be knowing no Prideaux. You speaks French?"

"Yes."

"I used to could but I done forgot it, 'cepting some cuss words." He yawned. "I's tired."

"Yes, so am I."

He twisted the neck of the lamp up, but it immediately flopped back with a grating creak. "Damn, can't get hardly no light 'round here, and that stove smell so bad."

"I'll go open the window some more."

"No, don't. It too cold outside. Long as we gots some air we be all right."

"I hope so."

He moved on the bed. "You know any Dotsons and Broussards in Lafayette?"

"No, I don't live there, you know."

"Oh."

"What's the Army like?"

"I hates it. You'm got to get up so early in the morning and the peoples is so damn mean."

"What do you do all the time?"

He pointed to an emblem on his shirt. "I's a sharpshooter. Some of the time we all goes out to the range and shoots. I shoots good. Oh, then sometime we gots them duties like cleaning them latrines and working in the kitchen. Outside of work like that it ain't nothing much to do but sit 'round and clean boots and guns."

"I knew a few people in the Army once. They didn't like it either."

"What you do?"

"Right now I'm traveling."

"Why you leave your home?"

"I don't know, I felt like it. I got tired of staying around there."

"Why ain't you got married?"

Eunice laughed. "Hell, I don't want to."

"Me and you could get married."

"Yeah, and sit up and talk to each other all day long?"
"I be good to you."
"No, thanks."
"I's lonesome and I needs a nice woman."
"Not me."
"Well, can I go with you where you's going?"
"I told you no. I can't be bothered."
"You doesn't seem to be bothered 'bout much."
"No, not around here."
"You strange. Come on in the bed." He took off his shirt and trousers. Eunice pulled off her dress and climbed in, turning her back to him. He turned off the light but still she could see the water stains on the wallpaper.
"Well, good night."
"You doesn't want to talk no more?"
"No, I'm tired."
"Well, how 'bout some loving then?"
"No." She pressed her head into the pillow. "I can't be bothered."
He laughed. "OK." Then he hesitated and put a hand on her bare shoulder. "You sure?"
Eunice didn't answer; she was already asleep.

In the morning she left, and for three more days and nights she wandered the winter streets of Lake Charles like some lonesome ghost. The wind whipped the dust on the sidewalks, and when it rained it came down in icy sheets. Every moment, to her, sheared itself into myriads of threads like fringe, each second tickling her brain with its eternity.

A drunken Irishman wandering in the wrong section of town bumped into her and whispered in her ear, "There'll be an earthquake in Japan, and another on the Isle of Man. No learning will reveal what we mean to conceal. It's a secret to the heel." He excused himself profusely and reeled off.

The streets were gloriously muddy and yielded underfoot like some young, fat-thighed girl giving in to the first tastes of love. Eunice walked softly, but swiftly, searching out the men with her hungry eyes.

Violence had been done to her, and violence must be given in return, so she had to put up with the men and their machinations. Most of their conversation was unintelligible, but she could discern the sense of their wantings by their eyes grown slightly watery with anticipation. Their knees would press to her thighs and their words were lost, but the now familiar low of insistence and lust carried all convergence of meaning.

She jived up and down the streets finding men and giving what was required just short of finality, just enough to abate the anger in her, then turning, she laughed at their throbbing frustration. In each of them she was looking for Blacksnake, not, as she thought, out of some vagrant sense of fidelity—that was in another realm and of no consequence. The wind howled around her and she realized she was still hungry.

She went to a phone and called X. L. long distance. When he answered she screamed through the bad connection, "X. L., this is Eunice."

"Oh, hi, baby. What you doing? Just 'cause you done run and left Snake don't mean you needs to hide from me. Come on over."

"I can't. I'm in Louisiana, Lake Charles. I think I'm going to come back to Raleigh. Where's the Snake?"

"Louisiana? Shit! You sure does let that dust fly a long ways off."

"Yeah, but how's the Snake?"

"Well, baby, you can't come back to see him. He done left town yesterday. He drive up the other morning and tell me he going to South Bay to see his Miss Sally Mae. Didn't even ax me did I want to go and he know my wife be down there. I doesn't think he felt too good."

"Well, I'll go there then. Do you know anyone there I could get in touch with to find him?"

"Yeah, baby. You go to my wife, Miss Mary. She make

flowers and stays down on Butterworth Road on the last place before the wharf. In fact, just down the street from it is the place where me and Blacksnake goes to gamble. But I wouldn't 'xactly advise you to go looking for him whilst he down there with Miss Sally Mae. She built kind of like a bull and she bellow just as loud."

"I don't care about any old Sally Mae. I want to find the Snake."

"Baby, you just forget about old Snake and come on home to X. L."

"Oh, hell, go 'head on." Eunice laughed and hung up.

She moved through the cold streets to the train station, got her things out of the locker, and waited for a train to take her back to Carolina. She was sitting reading a magazine when someone tapped her on her shoulder. She looked up and saw the soldier smiling his pleading, infant smile. "I just seen you down the street so I followed you. You leaving now?"

Eunice sighed and put down the magazine. He sat next to her and rubbed his hands on his kneecaps.

"Yes, I'm leaving."

Still his smile had not faded. "Well, can I come with you?"

"No. Why don't you just go on your way."

"I seed you around town after you done left me but you was always with some mens so I figured I better not come and talk to you. But now you ain't with nobody and I still wants to go with you."

"I can't stop you but I wish you didn't."

"Well, I'm going to anyhow. I likes you and I's lonesome."

"It'll be a waste of money."

"Maybe I can convince you to come back and live with me."

"Baby, you're going to be talking a long hard time to convince me of anything like that."

"Well, I'm got to try."

Eunice looked at him. "Listen, I don't want you bothering

me. If you're coming you're going to have to make your own way and leave me alone. I've got too many things on my mind to be worrying about every stupid thing you have to say."

He was hurt. "I ain't stupid."

"I really don't care what the hell you are, just don't bother me."

He slid his foot back and forth across the floor. "Look like you doesn't want me to come with you."

Eunice winced. "Goddamn, I don't. I've tried to tell you that."

He looked up at her. "I thought you was joking like when I axed you to go to a room with me."

"I wasn't joking then. I just couldn't think of anything better to do."

He licked his lips. "Well, I likes you, and I's coming wherever you goes. You ain't going to stop me."

Eunice shrugged and went back to reading the magazine.

She got on the train and he followed her, waiting for her to sit down first, then dropped down next to her. She kept the magazine high and in front of her face. Most of the time she either slept or read. The country was familiar to her by now, even in the cold of winter. But still she was awed as the old train fumbled through the forests and swamps.

The train passed through Raleigh. It was snowing and the platform where Eunice had gotten off last summer was wet and muddy. She thought of getting off the train and calling X. L. again but she knew he would only persuade her to stay, if only on the pretense of waiting for Blacksnake to return. Before she could make up her mind, the train had rumbled on out and hit the country again. In a few hours it would be dark, and they would be in South Bay.

The soldier turned to her. "What we going to do when we gets to South Bay?"

"I don't know what you're going to do, but I certainly know what I'm going to do."

His pleading everpresence did not constrict her anymore. He could follow her forever as far as she was concerned.

They arrived in South Bay late at night and Eunice decided to stay in the station until morning. The soldier tried to steer her to a motel, but she sat down on the first bench she came to and dozed.

fourteen

"Hey, it morning. What we going to do?"

The soldier was prodding her. Eunice got up, stretched, and walked out of the door. The cold bit through her clothes and the salt air burned her nostrils. South Bay was dead and people moved reluctantly. She trudged down back streets and alleys to the wharf section, the soldier always following.

She was upon the ocean before she had been able to distinguish it from the blue-gray land. It was soundless. Longshoremen on the wharf were loading and unloading cargo. Eunice found an ABC store, bought some gin, letting the soldier pay for it, and hurried down to a small beach between two piers.

Ships loomed like noble skeletons in the fog. She opened the gin and sat down in the rusted hull of a rowboat that had been abandoned on the sand.

"Well, what now?" the soldier asked as he sat down beside Eunice.

She did not look at him, she merely shoved the bottle into his hands, blowing on hers to ward off the cold. She took the bottle from him and drank again. Finally the warmth spread throughout her body and even in the cold she took off her jacket. She could not even hear the ocean lapping at the piling of the pier. Up above, the longshoremen bent up and down noiselessly loading boxes.

Eunice's fingers were nimble again. She drank more gin, took the guitar, and plucked a few notes, flinging them out to sea.

The soldier looked at her. "You shouldn't of brought that thing out here. It going to be ruined by the damp."

"Ruined? Be quiet."

"Well, it bound to get ruined. You know something else? You drinks too much."

Eunice defiantly took another swallow. *I drinks to keep from worrying, and I smile to keep from crying, because I don't want the people to know what is on my mind.*

Then she said, "I never asked for your advice, so why don't you shut up?"

"All right, but you still drinks too much."

"Christ, the trouble with you is you're too damn gentle."

"What you means? I's only trying to help you."

"Jesus!" Eunice exclaimed and jumped up. She grabbed her bag. "I'm going someplace now, and I don't want you coming with me."

"What is I going to do? I doesn't know nobody here."

"I don't give a Goddamn." Eunice walked off and the soldier sat in the boat tossing stones into the ocean.

She found the house at the end of Butterworth Road. It was

a white clapboard house with a roofing-paper awning attached to the front. Under the front window was a hand-lettered sign:

MARY MILLSON'S
ARTIFICIAL FLOWER SHOP

Eunice walked up and rang the doorbell. A short, thin black woman with neatly pressed hair came to the door. She looked out suspiciously. "Yes'm?"

"Are you Miss Mary, X. L.'s wife?"

"Yes'm. What can I do for you?"

"X. L. told me to find you. I came from Raleigh to find Blacksnake Brown."

Miss Mary looked at Eunice, and still with suspicion, let her in the house. It was dark and filled with sprays of plastic and paper flowers. She grabbed a handful from a chair and tossed them on the floor. "Here. You can sit here. Why you say X. L. told you to come find me?"

Eunice sat down and explained why she had come. Miss Mary seemed not to be listening; her eyes darted over Eunice, then about the room, and her hands fluttered in her lap as if she were wrapping the stem of a flower. Her eyes darted to the window. "Listen, girl." She raised a pipestem hand. "Who be that walking 'round out there? He ain't none of your'n, is he?"

Eunice looked out the window. The soldier was pacing in front of the house. "I don't know him," she said.

"Well, 'scuse me. I doesn't like no strange peoples walking 'round my place of business." She went to the door and screamed at the soldier to go away. He wandered back toward the beach.

She returned and sat down. Her hands started fluttering again, and her eyes roved over Eunice. "Girl, is you married?"

"No."

"How you come to know X. L.?"

"I got to know him through Blacksnake."

Miss Mary got up and bent over Eunice. "You's pregnant, ain't you?"

"Yes."

She pointed an accusing finger at Eunice's stomach and screamed, "I knows! Yes! You got that by X. L. and he done sent you here to show me up! Show me how fine a near-white woman he got since that fat nigger done left me! You knows, I done already shot and kill one of my hu'ban's. Now for him doing this I's going to kill him, too!"

Eunice watched Miss Mary, who was fluttering up and down the room in a frenzy, stepping on her flowers and crushing them out of shape. Eunice laughed. "Mrs. Millson, no. It's not X. L.'s, it's Blacksnake's, so don't worry."

Mrs. Millson halted in the middle of the floor and turned around. "What! You mean you got *his* baby? It be better if you had of done had X. L.'s. Glory rest my soul. You wants something to eat or drink?"

"No, thanks, I've got my own gin here. Do you want some?"

"You got some Old Hog? Well, I'll *say*. Yeah, give me some. Where you staying?"

"No place, yet. I've got to find a hotel or a room."

X. L.'s wife's hands wrapped themselves around one another and trembled again in her lap. She looked nervously around the room. "Girl, you can stay here long as you wants, providing you learns to help me make some of these here things." She picked up a torn paper snapdragon and waved it in front of Eunice. "Peoples just loves to buy them things so I makes them, but I thinks they's plenty foolish myself."

"Where's the Snake?" Eunice asked.

"Did X. L. tell you I's kin to Tom, I means Snake?" she asked. "Yes, girl, I's his natural cousin, but you'd never know it, we's so different. Me and him was childrens together down to High Points and one day we was playing in the pines and that Thomas Jeff'son caught one of them black coach-whip snakes and wrap it 'round his neck. You knows them coach-whip snakes fly out of the trees and strangles you, but old Thomas

Jeff'son just put that thing 'round his neck and that snake lay
there like it was his natural place to be. Ever since, all us done
called him the Blacksnake, but I still calls him Tom, and when
I's mad, Thomas Jeff'son Brown, which be his Christian name."

"Do you know where he is? X. L. told me he came here a few
days ago."

"Yeah, girl, he 'round town now, I thinks. But X. L. ought to
of told you not to come see him."

"It doesn't matter."

"Yeah, but, shit, he done took up with Sally Mae and it be
best if you just stay on inside with me and make flowers for
them peoples."

"I don't know. I came to find him."

"Yeah, girl, I knows. Let's talk 'bout it later. Where your
stuff?"

"It's outside."

"Go get it in here and wash up so we can talk some more.
You must be tired, child."

Eunice brought her belongings inside and took a bath. She
came out and Miss Mary was sitting at a small desk hunched
over wires and colored paper. "Girl," she called, "get you some
of this wire and papers and I show you just what to do. But
first I wants you to run over to the store and get me some more
Old Cushie Bag. That be gin. We needs something to keep us
going 'cause this flowers is a damned funky-assed business."

Eunice went to the ABC store and they sat down to drink
and work on the flowers. Presently Miss Mary got up, turned
on a battered radio, and started dancing to the music.

She looked over at Eunice. "Girl, I'm got to do something to
keep these old bones going. Them damn flowers work the shit
out of me. Get you another drink so's I can finish off the bottle
'fore old Johnson and her fool friends comes in here wanting a
taste. Somebody be bound to bring us more later on and I
don't mind hiding no gift, but when I buys it myself I feels
bound to give Johnson some."

Eunice watched Miss Mary, smiling at her shaking backside in a mirror. "Who's Johnson?"

"Girl," Miss Mary replied, still dancing, "you see her directly. She going to come hobbling in here with her nappy white head and walking stick. Her nose look like a damn shotgun and when she ain't here I calls her Poker Pig, but she an *old* lady so I's 'posed to treat her nice. She claim her daddy was a slave but it look to me like she kind of got mixed up and she the one who the slave. Naw, I's just shucking; she 'bout eighty year old and still like to drink. She hobble up the steps and sit down all day long talking and laughing like she just sweet sixteen, and she don't leave until it be dark."

They resumed their cutting, winding, and fashioning of flowers. The screen door opened and a tall, muscular Negro walked in, blowing heavily. "Morning, Miss Mary," he cackled.

"Well, Lord! If it ain't Shake-em-up! How is you, boy?" Miss Mary screamed as the big man grabbed her in his arms and swung her around. "I ain't seen your black ass since yesterday, damn you!"

"Damn, woman, you knows how busy I is." He turned around and looked at Eunice. "Say, Mary, who be this girl? She a new helper or something?"

"*Miss* Mary, if you pleases. Yeah, she just come from Raleigh and she going to be 'round for a while, I reckon. Has you been down to the warehouse yet?"

" 'Course I is." He cackled shrilly in a voice foreign to his bulk. "You knows, baby, John Lee and Rutherford's down there, and Black Gal and Arnetta's setting up there drinking and trying to get them to do a little boning. I been setting 'round listening to them but they been doing that for so long I knows their story."

"Shake-em-up," Miss Mary asked, "is you seen the Snake down there?"

He opened his big mouth. "Naw, baby. I didn't be knowing he back in town."

"That good. Eunice, I wants you to run down to the warehouse, it only 'bout three doors down from here. Go in and find Mr. Tall Boy, he run the place, and tell him Miss Mary want to see him directly."

Eunice put on her jacket and walked down the street. Just down from the shop she found a two-story building of corrugated tin set back from the street. Its sliding doors were open and inside she could see people sitting around an old potbellied wood stove. She smelled whiskey and frying fish and hesitatingly went in. Two men and two women stopped their conversation and turned around to gape at her.

"Do any of you know where a man called Tall Boy is?"

One of the women laughed and a man said, "Yeah, he upstair stacking stuff. Be back in a minute. Why doesn't you sit down with us and wait for him?"

Eunice moved a chair up to the stove and sat down. They stared at her. Six pieces of fish were crackling on top of the stove and one of the women was prodding them with a stick. The interior was dark and smoky and she had difficulty in making out their faces.

The other man turned to Eunice. "So you's looking for Tall Boy?"

The woman giggled again.

"Yes. Miss Mary sent me down to find him."

"Oh, you knows Mary?"

"Well, I started helping her today."

"Ah."

They sat in silence eyeing one another. A blue-and-white Ford bumped slowly down the mucky street, stopping for a moment in front of the warehouse, then going on. There was a scraping noise from above and a very tall, thin man came shuffling down the steep wooden stairs at the back of the warehouse.

Eunice stood up. "Are you Tall Boy?"

"You better know it, baby. Hey, looka *here*. Who be this woman? John Lee, where you find her?"

"She just walk on in like a lost goat."

"Well, what can I do? Anything, *anything* would be a pleasure!"

"My name is Eunice Prideaux and Miss Mary told me to find you and tell you to come to her shop as soon as you can."

"All right. Tell her I be down there directly. You want to stay here and have some fish with us?"

"OK," Eunice said and sat down again.

"What you doing 'round here?" Tall Boy asked, his mouth full of fish.

"I'm helping Miss Mary make flowers. Do you know a Blacksnake Brown?"

"Yeah, yeah, we all knows him. Least, when he got money either or plenty to drink. If he ain't got neither, I ain't got no use for that black bastard. No Negro, no matter how fine, if he ain't got no money, he ain't no friend of mine." They all guffawed and drank more whiskey to wash down the fish. "You got business with him?"

"I knew him from Raleigh. I heard he was here and I wanted to hear him play a bit on the guitar."

"Shit," said John Lee, "you wasting your time with that fucker. Now, old Rutherford here play *good*. He put Black-snake to shame."

"Well, I've got a guitar. Why don't he play some?"

The other man, Rutherford, looked up through the smoke. "You got the box 'round here?"

Eunice told him it was down at Miss Mary's. Tall Boy jumped up, scattering fish crumbs over the ground. "Good! I go with you to the shop now. I knows I can get Mary to close up for a bit and we can just jive 'round today."

They trudged back to the shop. A wind was rising from the ocean and they had to buck its force by inclining their bodies directly into it. They got on the porch and stamped their feet. As they went in they saw an old woman sitting in a chair talking to Miss Mary in a high, rasping voice. Another one, slightly younger and very thin but with large awkward bones, was making an attempt to sit daintily on a small chair.

The fat, old one was brandishing her cane. ". . . Yes, Miss Mary, I tells you it them white folks what's making things bad, them white folks is ruining us. . . ."

Miss Mary turned around to greet them. "Damn, girl, I thought you'd done given up on me. This be Missus Johnson and Missus Frook."

Tall Boy edged in front of Eunice. "Look here, Mary. This girl here tell me she gots a guitar and Rutherford want to play, so let's close up this shop and go down to the warehouse to party and raise a bit of sand. We got some whiskey over there."

"Shit, Boy, I'm got me some Cushie Bag here. What I want to go over there and talk to them old smelly down-and-out niggers that sits and shits all 'round that place?"

Old Johnson edged up in her chair. "Mmmm, Miss Mary, you just say you gots some gin 'round here? Bless my good Gordon's soul, I sure could use a little bit to aid my old-time rheumatis."

Miss Mary flashed a hot look at Tall Boy. "Shit, man, look what you done done now. Yeah, Johnson, pick you up a cup from the table and hold it out. I guesses I'm got to give you some. Frook, you wants some, too?"

Mrs. Frook angled her jutting body in the chair and patted her black wig with a coquettish flourish. "Awwwcw, yeaah, honey," she cooed, "I does believe I'll have me a little taste. Tha's so-o-o *sweet* of you, darling." She got a cup and extended an almost mummified hand toward the open bottle.

Miss Mary poured them a drink and said to Tall Boy, "Look, I go with you, but I'm got to wait for the White Hog to come 'round. Today pay-up day, you knows."

Tall Boy scratched his head. "Who the White Hog?"

Miss Mary laughed. "Nigger, that what I calls the *insurance* man, Mr. Talbert. He 'bout to come 'round to collect on my policy. I reckon it ain't going to take long."

"Yeah, I 'pose you'm got to wait. Here, pour me a taste of that for old time sake."

She gave him the bottle. "Boy, why you doesn't come down to see old Miss Mary no more? It used to be you would come down here and talk to me near 'bout every day. Now it seem like all you want to do is watch old Black Gal and Arnetta creaming after them sweaty niggers in the warehouse." She undulated her belly and patted it. "Now, what they got that so different from what I got?"

"Hush, woman." Tall Boy laughed and swung at her backside. "You know that my place of business. Beside, it too cold to be walking up and down the street for no reason."

"Man"—Miss Mary laughed—"I warm you up good if you come on down here."

Mrs. Frook rustled her underskirts and bellowed lowly, "Now, Mary, what *do* he be wanting to come up here when he can come up and see me enty old time he want to? Ain't that right, darling?"

"Ancient hefir," Miss Mary mumbled under her breath. "Onliest thing you good in bed for is to keep the sheet from blowing away." She looked at Mrs. Frook and laughed. "Now, Frook, he can't be bothered with you."

Mrs. Frook wiggled off the chair and tried to dance. As soon as she moved a foot and shook her hips, her hand shot to her back and she doubled over in pain. "Owwww. Oh, dear Lordy, the arthuritis got me." She smiled toothlessly at Tall Boy and her small ratlike eyes lit up. "Oh, don't you worry, sweet thing, you. Betsy may not be as fast as she used to be but she still can kick." She held out a bony hand again. "Please, I *would* like a teeee-ninsy bit of gin, darling."

Miss Mary grunted and poured her some more. There was a knock on the door. "Eunice, run and go answer the door. I hopes to Jesus it the White Hog and his old hot ass."

Eunice went to the door and returned followed by a gangling, pasty-faced white man whose receding hairline was compensated by combing long strands of hair over the top. He took a vacant chair and straddled it backward. "Well, hello, Mary. How're you today?"

Miss Mary walked over and shook her backside in his face. "Howdeedoo, Mr. Talbert. As you can well see, I's still shoving my stuff."

He laughed and wheezed. "Ah, yes! Is it cold enough for you?"

She sat down on his knee. "Mr. Talbert, with all these fine mens 'round, old Mary don't have to worry none 'bout being cold in the winter, neither nor being warm in the summertime."

Mr. Talbert's bulbous nose crimsoned. "Ah ha, yes! I guess you don't have to worry."

Mrs. Frook leaned over in her chair and cackled. "Yoo hoo, I doesn't have no worry either, Mr. Talbert, darling."

"Ah ha, yes. I guess you don't either. Mary, have you seen Laurine around lately?"

Miss Mary got off his knee. "Naw, Mr. Talbert, I ain't seen her for nigh onto three week. But I tell you what. She got an order for some flowers she ain't pick up yet. I go now and give her a call to see just what I can see."

He rubbed his hands together. "Yes, why don't you do that? Look what I brought, I know you like it." He bent toward his briefcase and pulled out a pint of gin.

Miss Mary turned around. "Lawdamercy! Mr. Talbert, what you want to go and do that for? That much Hog 'bout to put Noah back to floating on the Ark and if me and you gets to sipping I make you forget about Laurine."

He chuckled and called to her as she picked up the phone. "Don't tell her I'm here, just ask her to come get her order."

"Yessiree," Miss Mary called as she pulled the phone into the closet.

Mr. Talbert rubbed his hands again and looked about the room. Johnson was sprawled back in the chair, her fat legs barely reaching the floor. Her faded wrapper was bunched above her knees, exposing round white rings just above her kneecaps where her white stockings ended. She was staring at Mr. Talbert with slits of eyes. Tall Boy had edged into a corner next to a scratched mahogany table. Two of his ashy fingers were tapping out a slow, nervous beat. Mrs. Frook was resting tensely on the very edge of her chair examining her shiny legs.

"Well," laughed Mr. Talbert, "why don't you folks hold out your cups for some good stuff? You want some, don't you?" He extended the bottle to Eunice, who was sitting rather near him in a large padded chair and trying to concern herself with a movie magazine. She stiffened when he held out the gin to her in an obvious gesture of friendliness. He smiled. "Ma'm, won't you have some?"

"Yes," Eunice said and held out her glass.

Miss Mary came out of the closet. "Mr. Talbert, Laurine ain't at home. I can give you her number and you can go call her when you take it in your mind. Now give me that bottle and let me get drunk. It look like I ain't going to get no work done today nohow."

Mr. Talbert relaxed in the chair and handed her the bottle. "That's a girl. Take a day off to drink. I wish I could."

She went over and sat on his knee again. "Hell, Mr. Talbert, you know I shouldn't be doing that. If I does, what Miss Mary going to pay you with?"

Johnson lurched in her chair and waved a fat brown finger in the air. "That right, you mister white man! What you think us niggers 'posed to use for money when you always telling us to go 'round funning? We's hard-working peoples and soon as we makes a honest dollar you white folks come 'round grabbing it from us."

"Hush up, Johnson. Hush your mouth!" Miss Mary yelled.

"Naw, Mary, we's got to stand up for one another. I tells you my daddy was a slave and I's eighty-seven year old and it ain't *no* white folks *ever* get the best of Johnson. *No, sir.* And you ain't going to get the best of Miss Mary here, I's going to see to that, white folks!"

Miss Mary's mouth was agape. "Johnson, why you want to go do that for? Here we was having a nice old time and you come up with your aged ass popping off 'bout something you doesn't know a Goddamn thing about. And what ain't *none* of your business, too. Woman, we *ain't* living back in slave times. We's all straightened out now and I'm got to pay my *insur-ance.* If I didn't want to pay, I wouldn't of got none in the first place."

She looked at Mr. Talbert. "Sir, I's sure sorry this old-assed woman went and talked like that. She so damn old, if she even smell a whiff of liquor she got to open her mouth and drag down the white folks."

She pivoted back to Johnson again. "Woman, this man is one of the best mens I knows. He damn better than most of these black-assed bucks what been born 'round here. He only doing his job and I is glad it be him what's doing it 'stead of some other fool who *would* 'tempt to cheat me. So you just shut up and I buy you Coke Colas from now on."

She went to the desk, wrenched a drawer loose, and pulled out her checkbook. "Johnson, I wants you to *see* me give this here man my check. I's doing it with my own free will and it abs'lutely ain't *no* kind of pressure put on me by *any*one." She handed Mr. Talbert the check. "There you is. Now, let's get us another drink."

Johnson got up and hobbled out, calling Mrs. Frook after her and slamming the door violently. Mr. Talbert sighed. "Here, let's drink."

"Well," said Miss Mary, "I sure is glad that old cow gone. It would be, if she didn't get mad, she lay 'round here 'bout all the day, screeching and drinking and loud-talking. I ain't never seen a woman that old who could talk that long and that loud and still stay that fat."

Tall Boy moved over and took the seat Johnson had vacated. "Jeeesus Christ, mister sir, we's all sorry for that."

Mr. Talbert gulped his gin. "Well"—he laughed nervously—"everybody's entitled to get carried away once in a while. Mary, I've got to go and collect from a few other places. I'll leave the bottle with you, and I'll probably be back sometime this week with some more."

"All right, Mr. Talbert, you do just that. Good-bye, and don't you worry too much over Laurine. Maybe when you come back she be 'round here."

Mr. Talbert left and Miss Mary began dancing around the room with the bottle. Tall Boy grabbed it from her and pranced away. "Hallelujah for Mister Charlie," he yelled. "I sure as shit hope this one's rolling mill don't burn down. I'd sure miss him."

Miss Mary sat down. "Girl, you see how the White Hog was staring at you?"

Eunice nodded.

"Well, girl, he come down here to collect his *in*surance but he collects a bit of pussy on the side. This here Laurine he talking 'bout, well, she one of his womens, and he sure do treat her right. She don't have to pay no money to get the same *in*surance deal I does, and he just went and bought her a car. 'Course, he got his own white family, a nice little wife and three childrens, but that don't stop him from coming sniffing 'round here on the side. Laurine, she ain't no good. She done went and took that car and now I believes she don't want him no more. But since he done saw you he thinking on forgetting Laurine. He sure a fool, 'bout as big a fool as white folks can be, and still he sure do treat a black woman good in all his foolishness. I always says, better to get you a white fool than a smart black man. Yes, Lord!"

"Come on, Mary." Tall Boy stood up. "Let's get on back to the warehouse and eat some fish. John Lee just caught them and they sure is good."

"Hell, it look like with all this liquor that I ain't going to make no kind of fool flowers nohow today. Let's get going."

They walked down the street and Tall Boy bent down to Miss Mary. "Oh, yeah, I done forgot. What you axed me down to the shop for?"

"Oh, I didn't have nothing special. I just wanted to see if you knowed where the Blacksnake was. You see, this girl's looking to find him."

He laughed into the wind. "I 'spected as much when she come in axing, but I ain't going to say nothing. Let's go in and let Rutherford get his hands on the box."

They went back inside the warehouse. The others were still there sitting about the stove. "Shit," Tall Boy yelled, "John Lee, put some more kindling on that stove. It cold as the devil's wife's titties outside."

They huddled around the stove laughing and talking to keep from thinking about the cold. John Lee put wood on the fire and broke out two bottles of liquor. They sat drinking, then Rutherford took Eunice's guitar and began to play.

"Man, you done lost your touch on that thing. Better give me another drink so I be too drunk to listen directly," Tall Boy said.

"Shit, man," Rutherford retorted, "at least I can do my bit. All you can do with your long ass is dance."

A car drove up with three men in it. They sat for a while, then one ambled over. "Whatsay, man," he said, slapping Tall Boy on the back.

"Where you been hiding youself, man, down in the Bottom?"

"Naw, I been hustling. Hustling, man." He pointed to Eunice. "Who this?"

"She a new friend of mine. Come on, set youself down and get a drink. We's celebrating."

"What you partying for?"

"Shit, man, I don't know. But we's doing it anyhow."

He motioned the other two men inside. They sat down to

talk as Eunice and Rutherford played the guitar. It began to hail. Eunice gave the guitar to Rutherford and walked outside. The blue-and-white Ford rattled by again and stopped in front of the warehouse. A big brown woman peered out of the window, honked her horn, and went on. Eunice turned around and standing behind her was the soldier.

"Hi. Why that woman send me away this morning?"

"I told her I didn't know you. She said she didn't want strange people wandering in front of her house."

"Why you say that? You knows me."

"Hell, I can't be bothered with you."

"I done come all the way from Louisiana to Carolina and you telling me to go home?"

"Well, I didn't ask you to come."

"So you shouldn't be axing me to go."

"What about when your leave runs out?"

"Hm? Oh, well, then I'm got to go back. But I wants you to come go back with me."

Someone called from inside the warehouse, "Hey, Eunice, come on back in here! A hailstone going to hit you on the head directly."

"Look, I have to go back inside."

"Can I go, too?"

"No."

"Why not?" he protested. "I doesn't know nobody in this town to talk to 'cept you, and I wants to come with you."

Eunice called to Tall Boy. He stepped out, holding his big hands on his head. "Who this?"

"This fool's been following me all over. Will you tell him to go away?"

Tall Boy took a step toward the soldier. "Man, I's going to have to cut you if you don't leave this woman alone."

The soldier backed off and walked away. The sky was darkening and the hail was bombarding the ground incessantly. Inside they opened more whiskey and put the last of the fish on the stove.

Black Gal and Arnetta had cornered two of the men who had come in and were leading them to the warehouse loft, giggling as they coaxed them.

"Damn," said John Lee, "Black Gal and Arnetta sure will take on any sorry black fools for two dollar." John Lee had wide shiny nostrils that dilated whenever he talked.

Eunice, still listening to the hail, absently took the guitar when Rutherford handed it to her. *You know the blues is a bad feeling, when you get them 'round the break of day. I looked over on the bed, where my baby used to lay. I ain't going to let you, baby, make no fool out of me. Someday I'm going to live just like you, baby, happy as anybody can be.*

Miss Mary turned to Eunice. "There, girl, you go 'head on and tell it. I knows what you be saying, and I says the same for that black bastard X. L."

The hail and wind were insistent in their battering and thunder broke in the distance. The wind was blowing hail in the warehouse and some of it pelted Eunice.

Well, I came to Raleigh to hear the wild ox moan; I like his cry so I took the wild ox home. But I ain't going to let you, baby, make no fool out of me. Someday I'm going to live just like you, baby, happy as anybody can be.

Eunice angled her body around to better hold the guitar and she saw two black figures silhouetted against the hailing sky. *I walked from Raleigh, I walked to Lake Charles, got to thinking 'bout my baby, I couldn't walk at all.*

The figures slowly moved into the darkened warehouse and the tallest one said with deep arrogance, "Waaal, what *is* y'all peoples doing? Gambling for Coke Cola, I 'pose."

John Lee and Tall Boy rose up. Eunice looked past Black-snake and kept strumming the guitar resting on her distended lap. *No, I ain't going to let you, baby, make no fool out of me.*

Blacksnake saw her and stopped. "Goddamn," he exclaimed under his breath, "what *she* doing here?" Then he went over and stood before her. "Hi! I believes I 'members you. Ain't you that gal from Raleigh what picks on the guitar? Come here a minute, I wants to ax you something."

Eunice got up and followed him to a corner of the warehouse. "What do you want, Snake?"

"How in all hell'd you get here?" he snapped. "Well, no matter, you's here and I 'spect you done took it in your mind to stay."

"That's right."

"Well, listen here. I just want you to pretend me and you doesn't know each other too well. You says hello, and I waves, but don't be talking to me too much if you be 'round here."

"What do you mean?"

"Shit, woman, I means what I says. I got things a little tight right now and I doesn't want to get beat up, either or kill. Is you got any money on you?"

"I have five dollars in my pocket."

"Well, give it to me then."

Eunice reached in her pocket and handed him the five dollars. He put it in his wallet and started over to Tall Boy.

"Why did you do that?" she called softly after him.

He ignored her. "Tall Boy, let's gamble some."

Miss Mary came to Eunice. "What he tell you, girl? Naw, wait. Come on, let's go on back to the shop. We got to get us some supper." Eunice picked up her guitar and she and Miss Mary walked out in silence.

As they were finishing their supper of oxtails and rice, Miss Mary turned to Eunice. "What'd that fool cousin of mine say to you?"

Eunice told her and Miss Mary laughed, sucking through a piece of oxtail. "Yeah, I knowed it. You just better stay in here and make them damn flowers with me. I'm got it in my mind to beat his ass when I sees him tomorrow, Miss Sally Mae or no. He shouldn't of done you like that. And listen good to me—don't you give him no more money."

"I can't help it."

"Yeah, girl, I knows how that be, but no matter. Don't give him none, and act to him like he do to you. You seed that Ford what come by here today? Well, that be Miss Sally Mae coming 'round to check on him. I believe she done already got wind of you, so stay out of that big mama's way. You so small she push you with her little finger and you fall to the ground. Old Shake-em-up be coming over directly to take me honky-tonking. While we's gone you just make youself comfortable and relax. There a television in the other room and I's got some comic books and newspapers you can read. I be back later on."

Miss Mary got her hat and coat and went to the door to wait. Soon there was a knock on the door. She opened it, slipped out, and was gone.

fifteen

"Come on go honky-tonking with us," Miss Mary said to Eunice one night. "Shake-em-up and me's going out in the country to hear old Snake play some. Girl, I don't know if I should even be axing you, but I loves the music and I knows you do, too. And shit, well, it be 'bout to do you some good. You don't go no place hardly, 'cept down to the warehouse and following old Rutherford on Sundays."

"All right, I'll go."

"Ow-eee, good!" She began dancing about the room. "Yes, girl, Shake-em-up be here in a minute. Get your coat."

They got in Shake-em-up's '54 Mercury and clattered down

the road. Miss Mary nudged Shake-em-up. "Say, honey, I's
hungry." She chucked him under his chin. "Come on, let's go to
that fish place down the road."

"Aw, shit, woman," Shake-em-up protested, "I thoughts you
wanted to hear some music."

"Yeah, loving man, but I wants to eat, too."

He pulled over to a small restaurant and they went in. "Dog,
woman," he said as she devoured the fish, "you is the hungriest
thing I done ever took up with. I wants to go and hear this
music. I ain't heared none since Noah axed me on the Ark."
They sucked loudly on the bones, then went back to the car.

The town was small and soon they were in the country,
surrounded by a thick forest of small pines. Eunice was
slumped silently in the corner, conscious only of herself. The
road was smooth, but soon they turned off onto a gravel side
road and bumped through the pines until the road ended.
Directly in front of them was a small wooden shacklike
building covered with peeling advertisements. Stanback. 666
with Quinine. Lydia Pinkham's. Coca-Cola. Pepsi-Cola.
Kremo. Old Crow. In the daytime the place was deserted but
now, in the night, the floor was shaking with music and people
were crowded in like flies on a dead cat.

Shake-em-up braked the car and turned the motor off. They
sat for a few moments watching the people. "Come on, Shake-
em-up," Miss Mary said and shook his shoulder. "I wants to go
in and dance."

"Hold your horses, woman, I'm got to rest a bit. I's full."

"Shit, man, I's so excited, I's 'bout to piss in my pants."

He looked at her and opened the door. "Come on then,
woman. I guesses we better go 'cause I ain't in mind to bail us
out. This car ain't no bathtub."

They struggled out of the car and walked inside. As they sat
down, the music made their bodies tremble involuntarily in the
chairs. Nothing was still. The tables rattled with the vibration
from the amplified guitar and the drums. Eunice looked

around the crowded, ill-lit room. At the far back sat Black-snake, beating on the guitar as he had beat on her. He was triumphant in a fuchsia shirt and blood-red-and-white knife-pointed Stetson shoes, shined so that the cuffs of his black pants were reflected off the tops.

Miss Mary patted Eunice on the back. "Girl, I hopes you ain't mad we brung you here, but I just likes this music. Come on, get you some of this Cushie Bag we brung 'fore I drinks it all. I'm in mind to dance till I drops dead tonight. Come on, Shake-em-up, I wants to *dance!*"

Before he could answer she had dragged him out of his seat and they were plummeting around the floor.

A man came up to Eunice. "You wants to dance?"

She was full from the food, and tight with apprehension. "Not now, thank you."

He came around and sat down. "I's Sam Bassett."

"I'm Eunice."

"You Indian or something?"

"I don't know."

"Well, I is. I's one of them half Oklahoma Indians. Cher-okee."

"Let's dance." Eunice got up.

"I thought you didn't want to."

"You asked me to dance, so let's dance."

She took a large gulp of gin and followed him out on the floor. Blacksnake started playing a frantically insistent boogie. Eunice let herself be carried by the motion of the music and whirled round and round, forgetting Sam Bassett, Miss Mary, everyone. She was tired, her limbs ached, but it became imperative that she move to the music as fast as she could. She closed her eyes and bent down to the floor, whirling, shaking, twisting. She snapped up and leaped in the air. The music beat faster and faster.

Blacksnake's fingers were flying up and down the neck of the guitar and he was grunting *Boogie, do the boogie, and when you do it, do it, baby, in Jesus' name.* Her hair swung back and forth. *And when you shakes it, shake it the most . . .* She shook until her bones seemed to rattle. *. . . and when you shake it, shake it, baby, for the Holy Ghost.*

There was no stopping now. Closer and closer to him she spun and trembled. The music stopped. Eunice stood limp and wet in the weak light. Blacksnake was staring at her. He plucked a long and whining note, set the guitar down as the note was still vibrating in the room, and raised his hand.

"You knows, peoples. Some folks thinks they sharp when they comes 'round raising sand, but I tells you it don't do *no* good. Yes, 'cause I'm got me a *new* woman. Fine and new, yes, have mercy." He angled his head toward Eunice and twisted his lips so only the diamond caught the light. "Yes, peoples, I tells you she *so* new I ain't even got a chance to taste her milk yet. *That* how new she be. Yes, have mercy!"

He laughed into the microphone.

A lithe honey-colored woman with strawberry-hued hair knocked Eunice aside and pushed her way up to Blacksnake. "Hey," she yelled, "Mr. Blacksnake, play me another boogie! Yeah, I *loves* to boogie. Hot damn, and it ain't *no* shame!"

He took her arm and drew her up to him. "What your name, pretty mama?"

"Ignacia Louise." She bent over and kissed him.

"Whew, baby, you better not do that too damn much. I's liable to quit right now." Still holding her hand, he bent to the microphone and looked defiantly at Eunice. "Ladies and the rest of you folks, *this* the new baby I was just telling you all 'bout. Now I let her tell you herself. Baby, is I *ever* taste your milk yet?"

She lurched forward and hugged the microphone to keep from collapsing on the floor. "Naw, naw, naw!" she screamed. "Naw sireee! And this sweet man going to play me 'nother tune to dance to, ain't you, Mr. Blacksnake?"

He looked at her and laughed. "You bet your life, pretty mama!"

He picked up the guitar but before he could make a note she grabbed him and pulled him to his feet. She whirled him around and out to the dance floor, shimmying, holding his hand so he could not get away. He merely stood there watching her and smiling.

"Oh, baby," she screamed, "I likes this, I *loves* this!" She jumped up in the air, screamed suddenly, and ran outside with her hands clapped on her head. People started moving around, laughing loudly.

Blacksnake turned around. "Where my baby go?"

Someone yelled through the laughing mass of people, "Man, your 'new' baby gone but she done left her hair. She bald-headed!"

Blacksnake looked down and picked up a strawberry-colored wig. "Shit," he yelled and threw the wig out of the door. "Goddamn nappy-head nigger womens. Shut up, *everybody!*" He walked back to his guitar and jerked his head at Eunice. "And what you doing standing there, woman, why ain't you dancing with your new man?"

Eunice walked back to the table. She was trembling. "Where's the gin? I don't feel so good."

Miss Mary was laughing. "Oh, Jesus, did you see the look on that nigger's face when he saw that wig on the floor?" The hair at her temples was frizzing and sweat ran down her cheeks. She put a hand on Eunice's arm. "Yeah, girl, you doesn't look so good. You better go outside and get some air. Wonder what the matter with Snake to make him act crazy like that?"

"Shit, woman," Shake-em-up said, "I doesn't know. I just hope he play some more."

Eunice went out on the porch. The pine trees were shyly troubling the light wind, hampering its course. She sat down and held her head. There were footsteps behind her but she was too tired to turn around.

"You is still my woman."

Eunice grasped her head harder. The breeze was refreshing and unusual for the time of year but it cooled her only briefly.

"Go on then, girl. But you know, well as I does, you is still my woman and it ain't nothing you can do 'bout that."

"Yes, I know."

"You gots any money?"

Without turning around, she handed him what she had in her purse.

He sat down next to her. "That better. Sally Mae ain't 'round tonight."

She looked up. She wanted to tell him to leave, but instead she stood up.

"Where you going, girl?"

She walked toward the path. "I'm going."

He leaned back on a post and laughed loudly. "OK, baby, but you can't get away from me. Naw, like I says, you's still my woman."

She began running down the road. He yelled after her, still laughing, "And it ain't nothing you can do to excape that, no matter how far you and that baby runs, little girl."

Eunice stumbled out onto the main road. It was wide and upturned; the moon reflected down the path she had come. On either side were the short pine trees and brush. Now there were no cars but still she kept to one side, hugging the trees and staying just off the asphalt. She slipped off her shoes and crept along. All she could hear was the sound of her own breathing coming sporadically and sending a sharp pain to her chest every time she inhaled.

Down the road, on the other side, she heard leaves crackling and a low humming. She moved behind a tree and watched a small man come trudging along, bent and carrying a full croaker sack over his shoulder. She waited until he had passed, still humming to himself, then she moved on, alert to every sound around her. She listened to everything and suddenly the silence exploded. All sorts of noises clashed through the forest. Owls, crickets, leaves rustling, animals in the brush. She stopped and turned a full circle, her pupils dilating in fear, to try and pierce through the wood to the source of the noises. She turned around again and ran into the center of the road with a gnarled stick in her hand.

A car came roaring out of the east, its bright lights on. She ran back to the side of the road. It went past her, stopped, and backed up. She saw Blacksnake behind the wheel. "Walk, woman," he yelled. "I's going to see my *Sally Mae!*" He gunned the motor and raced on toward town. Eunice screamed at him and threw the stick at the retreating taillights but it fell short and bounced, breaking the moon's reflection on the road.

She ran and picked the stick up. Other cars came down the road. The dance was over. Her feet were sore from walking on the rubble and she wanted another drink. But she hid in the brush until all the cars had passed.

When they were gone she climbed back up to the road and walked—how long she didn't know or care—until slowly the trees thinned out and she was back in the city. She was sorry to be back in the city because she had wanted to walk in the brush until she dropped from exhaustion. Her mind was as dry as the inside of her mouth.

In a gutter she saw a wine bottle. She picked it up and drank off the rancid contents. She looked around and found a few more bottles in a trash can. She sat down on the curb, surrounded by the bottles, and began drinking what was left and calling down the moon. It trembled and sank into her palm, softly white and thin as poor-grade tissue paper. She tried to take it in her forefinger and thumb, but the weight of her flesh caused it to disintegrate, and nothing but a whisper of steam was left on her cold hand.

She looked up and saw the sky turning to the corroded steel of immediately before dawn. She finished off the residue in the bottles and a hot anger rose in her, making her dizzy. The sidewalk reeled around her. She picked up the stick and wandered off.

Slowly the fire subsided and was replanted with a cold drive. She stopped and examined the stick in her hand. She nodded to herself and wandered swiftly down back streets she did not know. *I'm got to find my baby, I declare that ain't no lie.* She remembered the lyrics and mumbled them as she walked. *I ain't had no loving since he said good-bye.* She walked and walked and as she did her eyes roved the terrain; she knew what she was looking for and she knew she would find it but she did not know where. *I'm got to find my baby, I tell you it ain't no lie. I ain't had no loving since he said good-bye.*

She saw the red sedan parked in the street. Her anger made her reel as she approached it. It was parked in front of a small house and she ran up to the window. There was no sound inside. She circled the house several times, crouched and tapping the stick in her palm. Then she stopped and dropped the stick. She spat on it and ran off crying, wondering what barbaric germ made her wander so in frenzy. She ran into Miss Mary's and fell down on the couch, dropping off to sleep instantly.

part **three** *things'bout coming my way*

sixteen

The winter was long and viscous. Then suddenly spring knocked South Bay out of its lethargy. And one day X. L. came to town, bursting in to Miss Mary's with a wild gleam. He knocked her over, picked her up, and kissed her. She screamed, "X. L., you bastard, where the hell you been?" He moved in and spent most of his days at the warehouse gambling and playing his harmonica.

As it grew warmer and Eunice grew bigger she and Miss Mary began sitting on the porch with their wire and papers, making flowers. Eunice would have her guitar and a bottle of gin at her side and when she became too drunk and hot to make flowers she would sit and sing. X. L. would hear her and come down with his harmonica. Occasionally people would walk by and give them a dollar or two to play some special song. They would take the money and buy more gin. People began to emerge from their homes and stand around the buildings at the end of Butterworth down by the pier.

Blacksnake was perpetually in the warehouse gambling and drinking, but Eunice said little to him except when he came to her for money. He would amble down the street looking behind him for Sally Mae, call Eunice aside and ask for five or ten dollars, always giving the excuse he was broke, then ask how she was doing, laugh, and wander back to gamble. Eunice would hand him money, go back to the porch, take a drink, and sing some more.

One day Eunice, X. L., and Miss Mary were sitting on the porch. The day was warm and the ocean's smell was pleasantly strong. Blacksnake tipped up to the porch to ask Eunice for money. As he called her aside she glanced up and saw Sally Mae drive up. She got out, lugged her bulk up behind Black-snake, and screamed in his ear, "Goddamn, you black-assed motherfucking bastard. This time I'm *got* to kill your ass!"

Blacksnake wheeled around and brought his palm, which was open to receive money, down across Sally Mae's face. "Don't call me no black-assed bastard, woman," he growled.

He shoved her away and she lunged up, snagging her fingernails in his cheek, cursing hysterically. X. L. began to play the harmonica, watching with his eyes twinkling.

Sally Mae bent over to pick up a stick lying on the ground and Blacksnake knocked her down. "Woman, will you *leave* me alone," he yelled, and kicked at her.

"Listen, you pissy-faced lying tomcat," she cried as she scrambled to her feet with the stick in her hand, "this mama ain't going to take *no* shit from a skinny-legged bandy-hen like you!" She started screaming and crying, and flung the stick at him. It hit him at the back of his head and he fell. She steadied herself, dragged him to the car, and drove off.

X. L. was doubled over, tears rolling down his face, choking with laughter. "Oh, Jesus, *Jesus!* Mary, did you see that woman whip his ass? I bet my britches he don't come 'round here no more. She do it better than old Jacqueline!"

"Damn right, I seed it. It serve him right, though, for doing Eunice the way he done done. I's glad *somebody* finally got to knocking something off that thick head of his." Miss Mary reached in her pocket and took out some change. "X. L., baby, go down to the store and get us some whiskey and some gin; we *gots* to celebrate this day. Eunice, come on sit up here and play some. I feels like dancing, I's so happy that nappy-head kin of mine got his due."

Eunice laughed. "You better believe I will."

The men from the warehouse came running up, with Black Gal and Arnetta loping after them. Tall Boy stopped at the porch. "X. L., what the shit happen?"

"Aw, nothing, Tall Boy, not a damn thing. Just old Miss Horse-assed Sally Mae done drove up and thought the Snake was co'ting this gal here, so she hauled off and whipped him. He knocked her down so she took to a board and beat him over the head with it. You ain't never seen such a scratching and cussing and fighting in all your days. Finally he done got knocked down by the board and she picked him up and toted him off in the car."

"Looka here." Black Gal nudged Arnetta and pointed to the ground. "That must of been his blood when he got knock by the board."

Someone brought beer, X. L. got the whiskey and gin, and they sat down to talk of the fight. Finally X. L. got up. "I better go make a run over to Miss Sally Mae's and see how old Snake coming along. I's still his natural partner." He got up and ambled off down the street blowing a fast boogie on the harmonica.

Back in Raleigh the bones of a rattlesnake snapped at the second neck vertebra. The carcass fell into the stagnant stream and floated off with other debris.

The people from the warehouse left soon. Eunice and Miss Mary went into the house to fix supper. They had it cooked and X. L. had not yet returned. "Wonder what keeping him?" Miss Mary mused. "Probably old Sally Mae got to beating on him, too. But if she do, I crack a vase over her greasy head and stick one of my fake flowers on her grave. Come on, girl, let's eat. I save some for old X. L. with his late ass."

They ate and sat down in the living room again to make flowers. X. L. came in and slammed the door. He was sweating. "Blacksnake dead. Woman, get me my supper and don't ax me no questions."

Miss Mary jumped up and brought him his plate. He gulped down the food, grunting and belching. Miss Mary kept asking, but he looked at her and told her to shut up. Finally he finished eating and with a big belch sat back in the chair.

"Well, I 'spect you wants to know what happen. I got over there and old Sally Mae with her big self was standing over Snake. He was laying on the bed, bleeding out of the back of his head. That board she beat him with must of cut him deep, and his face was scratched. I say, 'Come on, we gots to call the doctor.' She go to the phone and call him. He come over directly, take a look at the Snake, and say he dead from a cushion or something like that. Anyway, the board done made him lose hisself in the head till it finally done kill him. I just cast an evil look at Sally Mae and left back for here. That all."

Miss Mary began moaning and Eunice slipped out of the room. She walked into the back room, flung open the closet door, grabbed her clothes, and threw them on the bed. Then she rolled them up and stuffed them into her bag.

In a corner of the room was her guitar. She shook it until the rattles fell out, and ground them underfoot. Then she rested it on her lap and ran her fingers over the light nick marks, most of them made by Blacksnake when he had used it, plucking, strumming, and making it into a new being totally under his command.

Eunice sat on the bed and began to play. The notes slid out softly at first, whining their way around the room and softly dissipating into others. Her voice felt for the notes, soft as they were. *They says when a man gets the blues, he catch a train and rides, and when a woman gets the blues, she hang her head and cries, but when this woman gets the blues, she puts on her black wings and flies.*

Her forehead twisted into wrinkles, one eyebrow arched, and the notes began to rush out, each clouting the heels of the other like a cavalry at the sound of charge. *Yes, my black wings take me 'bout anywhere I want to go, they take me 'bout anywhere I want to go, but they just won't take me to the heart of my good man, and that's the onliest place I want to go.*

She gathered up her things and walked into the other room. Miss Mary looked up in surprise. "Where *you* going, girl?"

"I'm going back to Raleigh."

"But why you wants to go there? You ain't got nothing left there no more."

"Yes, Snake's mama's there."

Eunice smiled and walked out.

It was about a mile from the train station to the house. Eunice got off and began walking down the railroad tracks until they converged on Washington Street. There were no sidewalks in this section of town. The dirt streets had deep gouges cut in them for gutters, and flowering weeds for curbs. The people had lain planks across the roadcuts for walkways to their houses. In the cuts there were stagnant water and debris, and the children would hide under the planks playing games.

Eunice called out to them and they stopped, their eyes round. They did not answer her, but just stared, angry at her alien presence. They did not stop to consider words, but ran back under the planks to splash in the water.

Eunice walked on. Dark clouds clotted in the sky; the heat was like a heavy garment. She wanted to sit down and rest, take off the heat and the child in her stomach, and join the children playing, but she kept on walking. She clapped her hand to her stomach. *If I could call back five years, I would go places you could never name, then I would go and give those places my own name.*

But now, everything was named. Even the approaching storm. And an Orphic image danced and sang before her on the red road.

I woke up this morning, same thing on my mind, I was thinking about my my baby, used to treat me so nice and kind. Don't your home look lonesome, biscuit roller gone, don't you home look lonesome, biscuit roller gone; bet you ain't had no feeling, baby, even being alone.

The clouds thickened. *Sweet mama, you looks so lonesome and cold, your man done left you carrying a new load.*

As she turned down the road to Mama's house she knew that Blacksnake was coiled in her and pressing for release. The thought of that and the weight of her remembrance made her again want to sit down and set down everything for good, so the baby would not have to sing the blues of his father. *Sometimes I wish I had never been born, then I would not be here to be worrying and I would not have a chance to know what is going on.* But it had to be, and it had to be Eunice to teach him. Her first lesson would be the very act of giving life, giving him the chance to wish he had never been born. He would grow up knowing the intimacy of the earth she had learned so late. *Yes, it's gone down, Daddy, gone down to the end, but you better believe it's all coming right back up again.*

Mama's house was near the end of the road, dirty yellow with a wild tumble of weeds sprouting around it. It stood quietly hiding the setting sun, exposing only heavy purple clouds. Suddenly, lightning cracked above and it began to rain. *Weeping and crying, tears falling to the ground; and when I got to the end I was so worried down.*

Eunice took off her shoes and trudged up the road in the rain.

"Yes, it's gone down, Mama, it's gone down to the end, but, Lord, you know it's all coming back up again. So smile, black man, smile your sweet smile, 'cause there's a beat in my belly that will make you cry in a while.

People were running up and down the street, humped over trying to escape the rain, some calling to her: "Hey, girl, you going to get wet out there like that. Better get inside 'fore you drop what you got right in the mud."

Eunice stood there facing the doorway, letting the tears run down to the mud. *Yes, Mama, I feel like crying and I feel like lying down; I feel like driving myself right through this ground.* The sky was curded black with clouds and trembling with thunder. *Black Daddy, yes, you was so sweet, but you have gave me too much good pig meat. Yes, you made me go weeping and crying with tears falling to the ground, and when I got to the end, I was so worried down.*

The sky vomited again; lightning struck and shook the ground. She ran up the steps to the porch. *When I left my home this morning, you know I left my little baby crying, she say yonder go, yonder go that loving man of mine.*

"Mama! Mama Brown, come here!"

Mama opened the door and crept out. Black and wizened, she grasped a Maxwell House coffee can in one hand, and spit brown tobacco juice in it. Her snow-white hair was squared out and plaited firmly in short braids. "What you want, child?"

I feel like crying, Mama, and I feel like lying down, and I feel like driving myself right through this ground.

"I say what you wants, child?"

My man, he don't have no trouble, he don't have to worry none; because my man, he is his mama's seventh son.

Through the noise of the rain and thunder, Eunice screamed, "Mama, I come to you!"

Mama, I feel like crying.

Mama's eyes were almost completely closed by small folds of skiñ, but she squinted them open. "I ain't hardly got no sight, girl. Who you be?"

And I feel like lying down, Mama.

"Mama Brown, Snake's dead!"

"My Blacksnake can't do nothing but play music. He my boy, but he bad."

"Blacksnake's dead, Mama; and I have his baby."

Mama.

"Yeah, he a bad old boy. Can't make nothing but music."

"Mama, I have his baby, can I stay with you?"

Lord, and when I got to the end, I was so worried down.

"Child, you got his baby? Well, glory be. He a bad boy, ain't he, but he make music, too."

"Mama, can I stay with you until I have his baby?"

"Go 'head on in this house, child. You ain't got no business out in the rain with a baby."

Mama turned and went back into the house.

Eunice picked up her bag and guitar and closed the door to the storm.